TOUCH

What Reviewers Say About Kris Bryant's Work

Forget Me Not

"Told in the first person, from Grace's point of view, we are privy to Grace's inner musings and her vulnerabilities. ...Bryant crafts clever wording to infuse Grace with a sharp-witted personality, which clearly covers her insecurities. ...This story is filled with loving familial interactions, caring friends, romantic interludes and tantalizing sex scenes. The dialogue, both among the characters and within Grace's head, is refreshing, original, and sometimes comical. *Forget Me Not* is a fresh perspective on a romantic theme, and an entertaining read."—*Lambda Literary Review*

"...She has a way of giving insight into the other main protagonist by using a few clever techniques and involving the secondary characters to add back-stories and extra pieces of important information. The pace of the book was excellent, it was never rushed but I was never bored or waiting for a chapter to finish... this epilogue made my heart swell to the point I almost lunged off the sofa to do a happy dance."—*Les Rêveur*

Whirlwind Romance

"Ms. Bryant's descriptions were written with such passion and colourful detail that you could feel the tension and the excitement along with the characters…"—*Inked Rainbow Reviews*

Taste

"[*Taste*] is an excellent traditional romance, well written, well conceived and well put together. Kris Bryant has given us a lovely warm-hearted story about two real human beings with whom we can genuinely engage. There is no melodrama, no overblown angst, just two women with an instant attraction who have to decide first, how to deal with it and second, how much it's worth."—*Lesbian Reading Room*

"*Taste* is a student/teacher romance set in a culinary school. If the premise makes you wonder whether this book will make you want to eat something tasty, the answer is: yes."—*The Lesbian Review*

Jolt

"[*Jolt*] is a magnificent love story. Two women hurt by their previous lovers and each in their own way trying to make sense out of life and times. When they meet at a gay and lesbian friendly summer camp, they both feel as if lightening has struck. This is so beautifully involving, I have already reread it twice. Amazing!"
—*Rainbow Book Reviews*

Visit us at www.boldstrokesbooks.com

By the Author

Jolt

Whirlwind Romance

Just Say Yes: The Proposal

Taste

Forget Me Not

Touch

Writing as Brit Ryder

Shameless

TOUCH

by
Kris Bryant

2018

TOUCH
© 2018 BY KRIS BRYANT. ALL RIGHTS RESERVED.

ISBN 13: 978-1-63555-084-9

THIS TRADE PAPERBACK ORIGINAL IS PUBLISHED BY
BOLD STROKES BOOKS, INC.
P.O. BOX 249
VALLEY FALLS, NY 12185

FIRST EDITION: JANUARY 2018

THIS IS A WORK OF FICTION. NAMES, CHARACTERS, PLACES, AND INCIDENTS ARE THE PRODUCT OF THE AUTHOR'S IMAGINATION OR ARE USED FICTITIOUSLY. ANY RESEMBLANCE TO ACTUAL PERSONS, LIVING OR DEAD, BUSINESS ESTABLISHMENTS, EVENTS, OR LOCALES IS ENTIRELY COINCIDENTAL.

THIS BOOK, OR PARTS THEREOF, MAY NOT BE REPRODUCED IN ANY FORM WITHOUT PERMISSION.

CREDITS
EDITOR: ASHLEY TILLMAN
PRODUCTION DESIGN: SUSAN RAMUNDO
COVER DESIGN BY DEB B.

Acknowledgments

Every book tells a story. It's an opportunity to weave imagination, realism, and dreams into one tiny package. As women, we are nurturing and have this desire to help and heal people. When I was little, I wanted to be a doctor but realized that I simply didn't have the stomach for it. I've broken seven bones, have had four surgeries and numerous stitches, so I decided to combine all of my experiences and write a book about the process of healing—from the frustration of incapacitation to the glory of recovery. Only this time I took it a step further than anything I've experienced and weaved a little romance into this story.

Thank you, Fiona Riley, for educating me on physical therapy. Having gone through it a time or two, I needed to know all the reasons why it's important instead of bitching about the repetition of exercises. It was nice to have your expertise handy. Also, thank you, Kelly Harris, for being my in-town consultant. Hopefully, the next time we meet, it will be just to hang out and not me asking you a thousand questions.

My heart swells for my beta readers—Maggie Cummings and Nadine Godsoe. I know we were pushed for time to get this book ready for Women's Week 2017, and I really put the pressure on both of you. Thank you for dropping everything in your lives to cater to my whims. We got it done!

I want to squeeze KB Draper for her help and advising me NOT to put an alien in this story. We met at Grinders one night and worked through the plot like responsible writers—for about five minutes. That was all I needed. I love you, my friend. M. Ullrich is just as fabulous with her advice. Thank you for being available 24 hours a day—even when you are sleeping and you answer me early on your days off.

Bold Strokes Books always takes a chance with me and I appreciate their faith in my writing. I started this whole process completely wet behind the ears and I've grown over the past three years with their guidance and mentoring. The team behind the scenes is fantastic. We couldn't be this successful without everybody working together.

Cali—One day I'll listen and learn from you and all of your editing wisdom. I really do try to remember everything. Except for the oxford comma. That asshole gets me every time. Thank you for sticking with me though. I can actually see you rolling your eyes and smirking at me right now. You know you love me. You know I love you back.—Champ

To all of the readers out there—thank you for your support. Every review, every email, every FB message means the world to me. Truly. I put my heart out there time and time again with every book I write, and your support and appreciation fills it right back up. You are the most important people in this journey.

Chapter One

"Why does my new patient look like she's a lot older than twelve?" I ask my boss. I catch a glimpse of a lone woman sitting inside the examination room, her head down, her left leg in a removable cast. My boss motions for me to follow her into her office and hands me a file, but waits for me to process the information before she speaks. When my mouth drops open and I turn to her, she starts explaining.

"Okay, so she's twenty-eight, but she's here for a very good reason," she says. I stare at her until she continues. "I need you to do this as a favor." My boss, Gloria Bauer, knows I will do anything she asks, even if I want to scream and throw a tantrum. She explains that the patient is the daughter of her best friend from college and even though I have a dozen questions, I bite my tongue and nod. "She's kind of a pain in the ass. That's why I'm pairing you up. I guess I owe you lunch."

"Don't be silly," I say. Her smile is a mixture of a thank you and a touch of smugness. "This is at least a dinner. A really expensive one. One with wine and candles. And you should buy me chocolate. The fancy ones with liqueur made by a chocolatier whose name I can't pronounce." I turn on my heel and leave her office before she has a chance to respond. We both know this is a big favor. I stopped working with athletes years ago. Now I only work with children. I take a deep breath before I enter the room where my latest patient is sprawled on the examination table.

"Hi, Elizabeth. I'm Dr. Hayley Sims. It looks like I'll be working with you for the next five or six weeks." Her body language tells me she's as excited about this as I am. She leans back on her elbows and looks at me with the bluest eyes I've ever seen. The corner of her mouth slides into a smirk as she looks me up and down. Her appraising nod makes me grit my teeth.

"Call me Stone. Nobody calls me Elizabeth." She reaches down and plays with the side of the paper that's stretched over the examination table. The smile's there, but it doesn't reach her eyes. They're piercingly angry. I stop myself from releasing a sigh. Her problems are definitely worse than mine. I quickly and quietly review her file in front of her. Her doctor's notes are fairly extensive and as much as I want more time to study them, I know I need to assess Stone and make a decision on my own.

"So Elite is your second choice after the team therapist. What happened at the other place? Why did you leave?"

"The guy was an ass. He didn't even look me over, he looked at my X-rays, read my report, and said I'd never play hockey on a professional level again." Stone's cheeks were blotchy. She was getting angry. "So, Doc, are you going to say the same thing?"

"You can call me Hayley. And I have no idea why he would say that. Rehabilitation is a two-way street. It depends on you more so than on us. Once I can evaluate you and see where you are in the healing process, I can give you my opinion," I say.

"Are you a real doctor or just Gloria's assistant?" She's so dismissive of me. My defenses go up immediately.

"Are you a real hockey player or just the Zamboni driver?" I shoot back. I can't believe I came up with the name for that machine for the correct sport. I've never watched a hockey game in my life.

Stone raises her eyebrow at me. She's attacked my profession and I've attacked hers. "No offense, Doc. You just seem really young, vague, and unorganized. I've been around a lot of doctors and you lack their natural confidence. You seem more like an assistant or a nurse."

What did I do to deserve this? I stare at her for a minute and try to come up with something professional to say, even though I want to call her an asshole and explain to her that I no longer work with athletes because they are condescending. I also want to race into my office for my framed degrees, but I refrain. "Assistants and nurses are just as important to the medical field. For your information, yes, I'm an actual doctor with an actual degree. Gloria hired me knowing all of my qualifications. How about I take a look at you? Oh, unless you want me to grab our company directory so you can see photos of everybody and pick somebody more confident to be your doctor." I shrug at her like it's no big deal. I hate that I let her get under my skin so quickly.

Her eyes get wide. "I'm sorry. I kind of have a bad attitude lately."

I nod in acceptance of her apology. "Okay, now that we've got that out of the way, why don't you tell me what happened and how you got your injuries?" I wheel over a chair to sit in front of her. She sits up and watches as I gingerly remove the boot and bandages on her left leg. A fibula break is a tough one, but I'm more concerned about her fractured ankle.

"My car decided to wrap itself around a tree," she says with indifference, but she can't hide the bitterness in her voice.

"With a little help? Or just on its own?" Those heated, expressive eyes glare at me, but the smile's still firm on her face. Now we're in a staring contest. I want to smile because she doesn't know how good I am at this game; I work with children eight hours a day. We both wait. I'm the epitome of patience. She is a body of barely controlled anger. I understand why my boss wants me to work with her.

"I dropped my phone on the floor and took my eyes off of the road for a few seconds." She shrugs. I nod, even though I don't understand the need to text all of the time.

"Well, let's see what we are going to work with. Can you lie all the way back?" She slides back so that her leg is completely on the examination table. "Your hard cast was removed yesterday?" She nods. I carefully remove the rest of the dressing so I can look at the injury and the work already performed on it. "The surgeon did a great job on this." There will be minimal scarring. "How does your ankle feel?" I gingerly move it to feel the flexibility in her tendons and get a general idea of mobility of the joint. It's not as stiff as I thought it would be.

"Like it wants to explode." She wipes a tear away. I pretend not to notice. "I feel hopeless. Maybe it's time to hang up the skates." Her tone is sarcastic, but laced with sadness. I can feel her body heat before I even touch her uninjured ankle to get her attention. She looks up at me.

"You're not hopeless. Based on the notes from your doctor and the flexibility without a lot of pain in your ankle, I think you have a good shot at making a full recovery. We'll get you back to where you were sooner than you think. I promise." I see a flicker of hope in her eyes and I can't help but smile. "I just need you to do everything I say. If you don't feel it's the right thing, then talk to me. Can you promise me that?"

"I'm supposed to do everything you say? Is that how you get all the women, Doc?" At least the smile on her face seems genuine now.

"No, just the one I'm engaged to," I say.

She laughs. "Touché. Off the market."

I'm glad we got that settled. Now maybe we can get down to business. "Because of the extent of your injury and the fact that I'm sure you want to get back into conditioning for the upcoming hockey season, I want you here five days a week. Will getting to Elite be a problem for you? I mean, do you have somebody who can drop you off and pick you up?" She nods. "We'll start with some measurements and some simple stretching exercises today. I want to see what you're capable of. I'll send you home with some exercises, too. Do you have any questions for me?" I almost can't look at her. I'm surprised at my reaction to her. She's everything I'm normally not attracted to—athletic, tall, and cocky. I can't help but compare her to my fiancée who is Stone's polar opposite with long blond hair, brown eyes, and a petite frame. Alison is five foot three, whereas Stone brushes the six foot mark, according to her records. She's got me beat by at least four inches, even leaning on her crutches. I roll the chair over to the desk as if I'm taking notes, but it's really an excuse to get away from her. A hopeful Elizabeth Stone is incredibly sexy.

"So why are you going to help me? I thought for sure Gloria was going to work on me."

"I'm one of two pediatric therapists here at Elite. I'm helping you because my boss wants me to. She knows that I can work with all types of people and children tend to be the most difficult."

Stone busts out laughing. "You're brutally honest. Brutally." She shakes her head. "I know, I know. I'm moody and difficult to work with, but I feel like this whole thing happened because of a stupid text. Thank you for making me feel like I've got a shot at getting back on the ice where I belong. I promise that I'll try." Usually this is the time my patient wants to hug me or high five me, but there's a different energy in this room. I feel like I have to keep a front between us. Even though I'm going to get married in less than three months, I feel a small quiver in my stomach. That would be a good sign if I was single, but I'm not, and my reaction to her is unsettling.

"I'm glad to hear your attitude. It will make a world of difference. How about late afternoons from about three thirty to five? Will that work for you?" Again, I avoid eye contact and focus on jotting down notes in her file.

"Perfect. I can sleep in as late as I want to," she says.

I somehow think that someone on a professional hockey team is anything but lazy. I'm fascinated by why she's trying to make herself sound indolent, when clearly we both know she's not. I play along. "Just make sure to be here on time and do the exercises I give you to do at home. We need to get your ankle strong enough to support your weight again. We both want you out on that ice as soon as possible."

Chapter Two

My favorite part of the day is my drive home. Some people hate rush hour traffic because they just want to get home to their frantic lives of racing around and utilizing every waking minute. I take the time to decompress and think about my patients. Today, I can't stop thinking about Stone. She has so many layers and walls built up. Her injury is extensive, but not irreparable. The way her face lit up when I told her I didn't see any reason why she wouldn't be in good shape at the beginning of the season was a beautiful sight. She might miss several hockey practices, but getting her leg ready is far more important than learning how to execute plays. Gloria told me Stone has been playing hockey since she was four years old. I'm sure she will catch up quickly.

Alison's ring tone blasts through my car's stereo speakers. Her call startles me out of my daydream, but I'm happy to hear from her, especially when I'm not expecting it. "Hey, babe."

"Hi. I just wanted to let you know that I'm home and we got our invitations back from Meredith. They turned out well." I smile. Since the moment we started planning our wedding, Alison's been leaving a lot of the busy work up to me even though they're her decisions, too. Personally, I would love to run away and elope, but my family would be crushed. Plus, Alison has always dreamed of the fairytale wedding.

"Great. We'll probably need to get them out by next week. That way people can start planning their fall schedules." I can't believe I just said that. About seventy five percent of the guest list is Alison's friends and distant family. Most of her friends are all doctors. I think there are a few lawyers in the mix, too. I have the most in common with the pediatricians. Our conversations actually last for more than five minutes. Even though I'm in the same field as most of her friends, I feel like a stranger when I'm with them. I grew up riding bikes and catching fireflies, her friends grew up riding horses and catching private jets for trips all over the world. She hates it when I call them her TFFs, Trust Fund Friends, but I can't believe Alison actually likes these people. I shrug. This is her wedding, too, so I need to play nice. It's only for a day. Never mind that it's my special day, too. At least I have a say in where the TFFs will sit during the reception.

"How are you home so early?" I always beat her home by at least an hour.

"My final patient of the day cancelled and most of the paperwork I can do from home," she says.

"Want me to pick up some food on the way?" Our condo is centrally located in the middle of some of the best restaurants in town.

"I'm actually cooking tonight so just get home," she says.

"Wow. I'm impressed. Okay, I'll see you in a bit." I hang up and resume my review of my day. I wonder why, out of all of the physical therapists in town including the ones who specialize in sports injury, Stone is at Elite Physical Therapy. The Vermont Gray Wolves should have their own therapist or doctor on hand to work with injured players. Gloria didn't tell me so I make a mental note to find out tomorrow. Most of the time, she pushes paper and doesn't work with patients. Consider me intrigued by Stone's story. I check the time. The flower shop on the corner's still open. On a whim, I pull into the parking lot. There's something nice about showing up with roses or tulips even though Alison isn't crazy about flowers in general. Neither of us like watching them die. I carefully place the bouquet on the back seat and head home. Thankfully, we have a garage. It's one of the few things we splurged on when we made the condo purchase.

Before I'm through the door, Alison greets me with a glass of wine and pulls me to her for a kiss. "Hello, love."

I hand her the bouquet. "I know it isn't your thing, but I was in the mood to bring some home." She takes them from me and finds a vase in the kitchen. "Tell me about your day." I hop up on the bar stool at the kitchen nook and listen as she tells me about the two surgeries she had today. One was a meniscectomy, the other was repairing and setting a broken ankle. Our professional paths rarely cross because I work exclusively with children, but it's happened before. I don't tell her about Stone. I feel like I don't have a handle on the situation yet. When Alison and I discuss patients, we never mention names, only injuries or, in my case, some patients with disabilities.

I really enjoy working with children. Watching them learn and improve every week is so fulfilling. I admit, I get teary-eyed when my patients heal and move on, but I always hear from them. Every year, I hang up their holiday cards on my office door.

"Can you set the table and pour the wine? I bought us a new red to try," she says. I'm not fond of red wine, but I humor her. She knows this about me, but continues to try. Give me a beer or water, and I'm set.

"Do I have time to change? I promise to be back in two minutes." The look she gives me tells me no, so I peel off my suit jacket and grab the wine instead. I slip my shoes off under the nook and untuck my blouse. If I can't change, I sure as hell will be comfortable. She leans over and kisses my neck as she puts the salad on the table.

"I promise to help take off those horrible work clothes after dinner." I forgive her.

Dinner is angel hair pasta with crushed garlic, sun dried tomatoes, and a splash of olive oil. I add a ton of cheese. Alison doesn't. She is thirty-six, fit, and a true health nut. Usually our dinners are carbohydrate free with protein and a salad. It makes me long for my once a month dinner out with my few work friends. It's the only time I indulge. Well, and any time I can sneak away at lunch, which is almost never.

"Why are we eating this decadent food? I mean, what's the occasion?" I ask.

"Can't I make dinner for my soon-to-be wife?" She's entirely too accommodating right now. I squint at her. Something is up. She holds her hands up in surrender. "Okay, okay. I've been invited to speak at a conference in Chicago, but it's the weekend we are spending with your parents in New York. As much as I love them, I really want to do this conference."

My fork clatters onto the plate louder than I intend, but my point is made. "Are you serious? We've had to rearrange all of our schedules twice just for yours. You just can't cancel. Our trip is in a few weeks." I can hear myself whine, but damn it, my parents have changed their schedules at least six times in the three years Alison and I've been together, all for her sake. "I understand your job is important, but we all have lives and careers to consider." Now I sound like I'm really throwing a tantrum. I change my tune. "You know, it's okay to take a break. When was the last time we actually got away and did something fun?"

"Hayley, come on. You know how important these conferences are to me. There was a last minute cancellation and Oscar Whitmore reached out to see if I could fill the spot. I told him I would let him know tonight."

"I should have known all of this was because you wanted something," I say.

"That's not fair. It all happened today. I was excited to get out at a reasonable time today and just came up with the idea to cook dinner. Can we please not fight?"

Truthfully, Alison is a workaholic. I knew this going into the relationship. Even though I'm hurt, this isn't unusual for her. "You're going to have to tell my parents. And I'm still going to New York," I say.

"Fine. I will. I'm sure they will understand. You have the best parents. I really am lucky to be a part of this family."

I know she loves them and they love her. I already know they will forgive her immediately. Because Alison is a surgeon, she gets all of the kudos from my family. It's annoying sometimes. I soften my attitude a bit. "I'm still going."

"I know and I agree. Thank you for understanding."

I cross my arms over my chest. I'm not going to forgive her so easily. She always knows how to break me down anyway, so I might as well enjoy the attention. "What's the conference about?"

"It's the American Academy of Orthopedic Surgeons' Annual Meeting. Thursday afternoon is the meet and greet and the conference is from Friday morning until Sunday afternoon," she says. She knows I'm going to ask. I hate asking and she hates answering.

"Is Blaire going to be there?" Alison's divorce wasn't amicable. I'm not worried that she'll sleep with Blaire, but that Blaire will turn crazy, again, and make Alison's life miserable, which makes my life miserable.

"Yes."

I sigh and lean back in my chair. "Do you need me to go?"

"No, babe. You go have fun in the Big Apple with your parents. I promise to be safe and avoid her at all costs." I frown. I'm not convinced. Blaire used Alison as target practice with all of their glass and china when Alison served her divorce papers. I can't imagine Blaire being sane now. That was only four years ago.

"I'm just bummed. I was looking forward to a weekend in New York with you and my parents."

"I promise to make it up to you. You know I'm good for it." This is a true statement. When Alison makes things up to me, it's nothing less than incredible. I just want time with her.

"How much paperwork do you have?" I ask. "Time-wise. How long will it take?"

"I don't know. Maybe an hour or so. Why?"

"I'll clean up this mess while you work, then I'm going to draw a bath." She hitches her eyebrow at me. "If you finish in time, maybe you can join me." She jumps and races out of the room. I laugh at her theatrics.

❖

The clock reads 12:03 and I can't sleep. Alison doesn't seem to be having the same problem even though her sleeping patterns are worse than mine. In all fairness, she did exert herself nicely tonight and I'm delightfully sore as proof. Our sex life has settled down a lot since we've been together. We're slowly trying new things in the bedroom. And in the Jacuzzi bath. Even though Alison is five years older than I am, she is in twice the shape. She runs when I sleep in, she works out during her lunch while I secretly eat carbs, and she enjoys eating quinoa. Nobody enjoys that. I hate the salads we eat weekly. I know she's trying to keep us healthy and alive, but every so often I just want to order pizza and drink beer and not feel guilty about it. I'm having an affair with fattening food.

After twenty minutes of sitting, I quietly get out of bed. I snuggle under a blanket on the couch. Remote in hand, I turn on a marathon of *The Walking Dead* even though I've seen every episode. I notice a box on the coffee table. Inside, I find our wedding invitations. I open one up and smile. They're nice. Not six hundred dollars nice, but Alison wanted them. She eloped the first time, so now she wants an elaborate wedding. Even though I have to plan it, her role is to swoop in at the last minute and change everything. I'll be glad when this is all over.

The invitations are more contemporary than I would have liked because we chose not to list our parents. Alison's father passed away years ago and she hasn't talked to her mom in forever, so we had to improvise. I feel bad that my parents aren't listed, but they understand since Alison isn't listing her mom. I file the invitation back in the box, knowing that I will be responsible for addressing and sending them out. I might even enlist the help of Tina, one of

Elite's administrative assistants. She's always looking for things to do. Hopefully, she can knock out most of them so that by the weekend, I'll only have a few left. She has better handwriting than I do anyway. I curl back up on the couch and try to block wedding anxiety from my mind.

"Hayley, what are you doing out here? Come back to bed." Alison is gently shaking my shoulder. I was finally asleep.

"What time is it?" I groan when she tells me it's only three. She pulls me up and kisses my nose.

"I don't like waking up without you." I follow her and let her tuck me into bed. She wraps her arm around my waist and, within seconds, she's asleep. Again, I'm awake with my thoughts. Stone won't leave my mind. I'm probably intrigued by her because it's been forever since I've worked with an adult. I promised to get her ready by the season, which I chalk up to an attempt at inspiration. She's strong enough to make it happen. It was just so hard to see tears in those giant blue eyes of hers. Tomorrow, I'm going to sit myself down in Gloria's office and get the truth about her.

Chapter Three

Gloria comes in, knocking after she opens the door. "My Keurig isn't working. Can I use yours?"

I look up from my paperwork, annoyed at the interruption. Then, remembering I want to have a conversation about Stone, I change my tune. "Come on in. I've got some chocolate donut flavored coffee if you want that instead." I couldn't be more conniving. She slowly walks to the sideboard, her eyes never leaving mine. "So tell me why Elite agreed to work with Elizabeth Stone, professional hockey player extraordinaire. I want to know what I'm getting myself into here." Gloria takes a seat across from me after doctoring her pastry smelling coffee.

"I've known her mother since college. I talked with her and Elizabeth is on the fast track to self-destruction. She's completely distraught over this injury and has been very difficult to work with. She made the Gray Wolves' own sports therapist cry after their first appointment. Stone's manager strongly suggested she look outside for a physical therapist. I volunteered because I know we can help her. You have the utmost patience and can keep your shit together better than anyone else. You're my best therapist. Even the kids who have a hard time facing their disabilities love you."

"How many other therapists has she tried? What's the problem other than her poor me attitude? Her injury is bad, but not necessarily career ending." I've seen athletes come back from far worse injuries and still have good seasons. Gloria leans back in her chair and sighs.

"You know how athletes are. They think their injuries are the worst ever. She's only been to one other therapist and she destroyed the room after one session. That's when her mother called me."

"What the hell happened there?" I start to doubt my own assessment of Stone. What did they see that I didn't?

"The therapist was some young kid and told her he wasn't sure she'd play hockey again. Not a great way to start the first session. Stone lost it and starting smashing her crutches into things." Gloria doesn't look concerned at all.

"You know how I feel about athletes. They are jerks and harder to control than kids. What if she pulls that with me?"

"Don't tell her she can't play hockey. Look, I know you haven't worked with sports injuries for the last few years, but I think we can work together and salvage this girl's career." She pauses to take a sip of the coffee. Guilt trip planned and now I'm packing for it.

"I'm not that good." She waves her hand at me in a dismissive way.

"You're my best. I'm serious, Hayley. What you've done here has been remarkable. I know I'm asking a lot of you to take on Stone, but I've known her family a long time. If she doesn't get better and improve her attitude, she will lose her job and all of her endorsements. We know what kind of downward spiral that can be." We both have seen our fair share of athletes whose careers crashed and burned because of their injuries.

"Thank you for telling me. That perspective helps. Not to be a total shit here, but why don't you jump back in and work on her instead of me? Your background in sports related injuries is far superior to mine, plus you know the family. That should give you the upper hand right away," I say. The chocolate coffee smells so good that I get up and make myself a cup.

"You know that I've lost my patience for patients." She pauses to smirk. "I really do prefer the administrative side of this job."

Which translates to she doesn't want to because she's the boss now, only eight years from retirement. I can respect that. "And I've a lot going on with the Children's Dream Maker's fund-raiser coming up." Next month, we're raising money for the local organization who grants critically ill children wishes. It's heartbreaking and heartfelt at the same time.

"How difficult is Stone? Truthfully. I need to know what I'm getting into." I hold my hands up to stop her from becoming defensive. "I'm still going to do this, for you, for the practice. I just need her history. And please tell me it's not because we are both lesbians." She laughs.

"Are you serious? I just need my best to work with her," she says.

I give her a look. "I don't see a problem with any of this. I just wanted more info. It's been a long time since I've worked with adults. I figured there had to be a good reason."

"If things get out of control, let me know. If I have to step in, I will. She's a good kid. She isn't used to being told no, but she's worked hard to get where she is. Did you know she was an alternate in the Olympics a few years ago?" I shake my head. I'll have to Google her later. "Yeah. Not bad if you ask me. Hockey is her life. I'd like to give her that back if we can." Gloria stands up and stretches before she heads to the door. "Okay, I'm out. Let me know if you need anything. When do you start on her?"

"We started a bit yesterday. I wanted to gauge her levels. I'm going to work on her Monday through Friday. She'll be my last patient of the day. If she can get here early, maybe I can squeeze some aqua therapy in. I trust she can swim."

"I'm sure she does. Ice, water. It's all the same," she says. She winks at me as she leaves my office.

I Google Stone's name and am floored by all of the articles that pop up. Tons about her successes, very few about her failures. I had no idea she is this popular. Actually, I hadn't given women's ice hockey a single thought before yesterday. I know soccer has blossomed in women's sports, but who knew about hockey? I hit the images tab and am instantly struck by those gorgeous sapphire eyes from thumbnail photos on the page. Her hairstyle has changed so much over the years. It was long, then short, then really short. I like the shaggy, messy style she has now. I read a few articles and am impressed that she went to Dartmouth. There are several interviews on YouTube and I pull up a few. She's passionate, friendly, and makes every single interviewer blush. The camera loves her. I shake my head and roll my eyes at her blatant flirting. I did get a glimpse of it yesterday for about two seconds, but mostly I was introduced to the brooding, sulking lesbian who believes this is the worst thing to ever happen to anybody ever. I pull her file and make a few notes. I'm interrupted when Tina intercoms me.

"Alaina's here," she says. I glance at the clock. I push back from the desk and slip my shoes back on. I stop in front of the reception area and grab the top envelope from the stack already piled on Tina's desk.

"Your handwriting is gorgeous. Thanks for helping me."

Tina smiles. "Thank you for giving me something fun to do. This is so cool. I'm so happy for you."

I think I'm the only lesbian she knows. She hasn't even met Alison yet.

I beeline it to therapy room A, which is for infants through elementary school age children. I smile when I see my tiny patient already playing with blocks.

"Hello, beautiful girl. How are you doing today? What are we building?" I drop to my knees next to her and watch as she struggles to stack the blocks taller than herself. Alaina is one of my favorites. She fell out of a second story window after climbing up on the windowsill and leaning her full body weight against the screen. Thankfully, a tree under the window broke her fall. We're working on getting mobility back after she dislocated her shoulder and elbow. The bruises are already starting to fade.

"Hi, Miss Hayley. I'm going to make this taller than you." She bites her lip as she concentrates and wills her body to stretch so she can keep stacking.

"Have you stretched the right way today?" I look to Matt, the other pediatric therapist, who nods. He gets my patients ready when I get lost in paperwork. I don't think she's ready for the miniature rock wall yet so, after a few more minutes stacking blocks, we head over to the soft, climbable zoo animals that are the biggest attraction of the therapy room. Judging by the way she is scampering over the zebra and hippo, I think Alaina's PT will be over soon. I'm sad, but glad to be a part of her healing. I work with Alaina for another thirty minutes until her session is over and spend some time with her parents. I like the whole family. They were the first ones to volunteer to help out at our fund-raiser for the Children's Dream Maker organization. We raise a lot of money every year as thankful patients and parents donate time and money to help us. It's an end of the summer carnival with fun things for kids to do including game booths and low impact bounce houses. We don't have rides because they are too much of a liability, but the kids have fun with the simplicity of what's available. Alaina's parents are in the restaurant business and are donating most of the food. Some of our patients donate money. It's open to the public, but a lot of our patients, existing and past, bring their friends and it's so wonderful to see. Kids being kids again, injuries gone or in the process of healing. The Children's Dream Maker organization sends over ambassadors with a few Dream Maker children who are able to participate as well. It's a feel good event on every level. I'm in charge of drinks, the kid-friendly kind only. The hard stuff comes out when we are cleaning up afterwards.

"I'm so excited to be a part of this," Desiree, Alaina's mom, says. The sincerity on her face is unmistakable.

"It's always so much fun. The kids have a great time and it's for a good cause," I say.

"Do you need anything else from us?" she asks.

I remember the flyers Gloria created and hand her a stack. "If you put these somewhere in your restaurant where your patrons can pick one up, that would be great."

"Oh, we can even pass them around the neighborhood," Desiree says. I refrain from hugging her.

"You have done so much already. Thank you," I say. If all of this goes well, I think this will be the biggest turnout yet.

Chapter Four

I'm actually nervous. It's almost three thirty and I know that Stone will be here any minute. Since our initial sessions will be mainly stretching her out, I'm having her meet me in therapy room A. Gloria said I need to work with her, but she didn't specify where. Matt will be working with his last patient of the day, an adorable eight-year-old who lost his leg due to a severe infection. Watching Davis walk with a prosthetic leg truly puts things into perspective. Maybe Stone will see that there are worse cases than hers. I grab my clipboard with the measurements and stats that we collected last Thursday and head down to the kid-friendly workout gymnasium. Stone is already there, sitting at one of the kids' tables, her cumbersome boot stretched out in front of her. I watch as she observes Davis out of the corner of her eye. I give her a few minutes, probably more than I should, so that I can watch her and gauge her reaction to him. When I do open the door, Stone looks directly at me, those blue eyes still blazing, but this time they are a little softer.

"Hello, Stone. How's the leg?" I ask.

"Miss Hayley. Hello. Look at how well I'm walking," Davis interrupts. He walks over and high-fives me.

"Davis. Look at you! I almost didn't recognize you with the way you were racing around here." I'm rewarded with a huge smile.

"I can jump now, too." He hops up and down and I can't help but clap. Children really are resilient. I turn back to Stone after he hops off to work with Matt again. Her face holds very little emotion, but I have to think that entire exchange affected her.

"Are you ready to get started?"

She nods. "I did everything you told me to over the weekend. I spelled the alphabet with my ankle, kept my leg elevated and on ice. I was the exemplary patient." This time her smile is sincere and it almost takes my breath away.

I stumble over my words a bit. "Fantastic. Let's get started. I'm going to start off with a deep tissue massage. This will help your ankle a lot, I promise, but you will hate it while I'm doing it. It's designed to prevent scar tissue." She gasps when I dig my fingers into her ankle. I'm more careful with her leg. I quickly realize that Stone isn't easily distracted when I chat so I stay quiet. By the end of the twenty minute massage, she's sweating and not in a good way.

"I deserve something special after that abuse." She groans, but then she winks at me. I roll my eyes, but I give her a break for ten minutes while I treat her to an ultrasound. It's painless and soothing.

"You were so right. I hate you and love you at the same time," she says.

My breath hitches at her warm and gravelly voice. "Patients get excited about the massages until they actually receive one. It takes a little bit of time to get used to them, but by the end of this, you'll be putty in my hands," I say. I avoid all eye contact because that sounded way more sexual than it was supposed to.

We exchange only a few words over the next forty-five minutes. Sweat beads on her brow. She has worked hard and wants to push herself even harder, but I have to pace her. We finish with the stretches and I tell her to lie back on the table for a cool down exercise.

"I know this is frustrating as you get used to walking and bending again, but you just have to trust me that I know what you need." Stone raises her eyebrow at me and I have the decency to blush. We're quiet for a few minutes while she rests and elevates her leg.

"So what happened to that kid?" she asks.

"Davis? He had a bone infection. He's been coming here for weeks and has proven to be one tough little dude," I say.

"Do you have any kids of your own?"

"Me? No. I don't know that we will. Alison doesn't really want them." I inwardly groan. I can't believe I just shared something so personal with a patient.

Stone snorts and then quickly apologizes. "I didn't mean anything by that. I'm just shocked. I mean, you work with kids and from what I've seen, you're good with them," she says.

I shrug. Before Alison, I wanted at least two. She convinced me that kids would be a burden and we would lose ourselves in the process. "What about you? Are you planning on having kids?"

She laughs. "Well, I haven't really given it a lot of thought. I've been pretty busy with hockey the last twenty-four years of my life."

"No girlfriend?" Again, I scold myself for getting personal.

She shakes her head. "No time really. Most of my relationships take place off season." That makes me sad. Her whole life has been hockey. I help her put her boot on, satisfied that the swelling is minimal.

"Okay, you're all set. Stay elevated tonight. Same time tomorrow, okay?" She slides off the table and grabs her crutches.

"Thanks, Doc. See you then." I watch as she hobbles over to the doorway.

I find myself still smiling minutes after she's gone. I understand why Gloria wants me to work with Stone. She's eager like a kid and just as unaware. I have a feeling she would push herself too hard and would reinjure her leg. Tomorrow, we'll have to talk about her limits. I'll draw up a timeline of where she should be in the healing process and when she can do certain activities. I'm sure she's itching to get back out on the ice, but she's weeks away from even trying it.

Chapter Five

"Why am I so sensitive to touch?" Stone is sprawled out on the table and I'm giving her the dreaded massage. I'm sure she thinks I'm trying to kill her.

"Your leg is still healing and you have to learn how to feel again." Why does everything I say sound sexual? "How did it feel when you got your cast off?"

"Unbelievably stiff. Is that normal?"

"Your leg was in a hard cast for weeks with zero mobility. Yes, it's perfectly normal and exactly what you needed to heal the bone. The hard part is done. Now we need to focus on getting your ankle to move your foot up and down, to the left, and to the right. It'll take time. I know it's frustrating, but you are kind of learning how to do things all over again." She makes a grunting noise before falling back on the table.

"I hate that this is taking so long," she says. I feel bad that this is only the end of the second week. She's entirely too competitive to hold back.

"How about some good news? I have two patients who are starting water therapy next week. I think that might be good for you. Are you a good swimmer? We would start off slow and just see how well you handle it."

"I learned to swim before I could walk."

"You have a swimmer's build. Why did you pick ice hockey over swimming?" Again, I'm getting too personal with Stone. Did I really just mention her body?

"I like going fast. I can swim fast, but only as fast as my body will let me. On skates, I can reach speeds up to fifteen or even twenty miles an hour. It's such a freedom. Besides, here in the northeast you're practically born with skates on. Are you from here, Doc? Did you skate any as a child?"

The thought is foreign to me. "I'm from here, but my passion growing up was always dance. I took tap, ballet, and ballroom lessons."

She looks me over. "That's about right."

"What does that mean? I don't look like a badass hockey player?" I grit my teeth and snarl at her. She laughs and playfully touches my arm. Her hand is warm and makes me inwardly shiver. Not professional, I scold myself. This is just friendly banter.

"You are entirely too nice to be a hockey player. I can't imagine you getting checked against the wall." I assume she means brutally crushed up against the side of the rink. Those checks always make their way to the news during the hockey highlight reels.

"Are you kidding me? Do you know who I am?" I'm rewarded with a hefty laugh.

"Stop. What damage could you do? You are so slight," she says. I shiver again when I watch her eyes slowly travel over my body.

"I'll have you know that I'm a red belt in tae kwon do, thank you very much." I put my hand on my hip and glare at her.

"Huh. I didn't think you had it in you to kick some ass," she says.

"You're not the only tough one here." I lift my eyebrow at her. "My father insisted that I learn some form of discipline, besides dance, and some self-defense. Tae kwon do was the answer."

"Do you still practice?"

"I haven't in years, but it's like riding a bike. I just need to get back to it."

"Why don't you then?"

"I'm kind of busy right now with patients and planning a wedding," I say.

"When is the big day?"

"October twentieth." I hand her the ice pack and tell her to relax for a bit. Today's exercises were hard, but she pushed through them with minimal complaining. She really isn't as difficult as Gloria portrayed her to be.

"That's coming up. That's the start of our season," she says. Sooner than I'd like. I take a deep breath. I really need to get those invitations out in the mail today. I keep forgetting to do that. I wheel over to the desk and make my notes in Stone's file. "Are you getting excited?" I frown because I'm not, but then I smile weakly at her.

"There's a lot going on so it's hard to say if I'm excited or stressed." At least I'm being honest. She grimaces at me.

"Where are you having your wedding? Where's the venue?"

Simple questions. I like that. "We are staying local, the Grande Theatre. Contrary to the name and place, it really is a simple wedding. I would have been happy eloping."

She nods. "Yeah, I'm all for running away, too. I've seen so many weddings in my life. My parents run Stone Orchard and it's amazing how many people want to get married there."

"You're kidding. I love that place! I actually was going there after work to pick up some cider and apples. I bake when I'm stressed." She laughs when I groan and smack my forehead playfully. "I should have connected the names."

"I grew up there. It's a great place for a kid. Forty acres of apple trees and barns. And it's just up the street from the practice rink," she says.

We're quiet again for a few minutes. I'm very aware of the silence and I can feel when she's looking at me. My pulse races. "So why do you go by Stone?" She leans on her elbows so she can face me. I forbid myself to look at her body even though that pose—one knee up, breasts pressed against her T-shirt—is sexy as hell.

"Coaches call you by your last name. Even the players do. Also, I've never acted like an Elizabeth." She pushes her messy hair back. "If you want, I can give you a tour of the orchard." We both look down at her leg in a brace and her crutch nearby.

"No, it's okay. You need to rest anyway."

Stone laughs. "We have an all-terrain vehicle. A golf cart on steroids. We can take that." I waver. I don't like for my personal and professional lives to cross and I think Stone might be a red flag in both. "C'mon. It will be fun. I promise not to monopolize your time." She looks so hopeful.

"Okay. If you don't mind, that would be nice." So much for listening to my own reasoning and all of the dangerous warning signs going off in my head.

"Do you want to just leave from here? Or is that Elite taboo?"

I don't think that's a problem. I silence the tiny alarms again. "I can drive. Is somebody picking you up though?"

She quickly types something on her phone. "Not anymore." I'm so happy I'm sitting down because the devilish smile she gives me is extremely suggestive. I quickly look down at my paperwork and write down miscellaneous notes in the margins to look busy. This is going to be a long evening.

Chapter Six

"You are probably so tired of apples, having lived here your whole life."

Stone plucks an apple off of a nearby low hanging branch, studies it, and polishes it against her sweatshirt. She hands it to me. "There are so many things you can do with apples. I love to bake and cook. The trick is to find different things you can do with them," she says.

"Do you work here, too?" I ask.

She laughs. "Oh, God, no. It pained me to temporarily move back when I busted my leg. I love my parents, but once you leave home, it's hard to return. In all fairness, my mom has been fantastic with me. It's just hard, you know?"

"Where do you live?" I ask.

"Why, Doc, are you into making house calls?" She playfully raises her eyebrow at me. I blush and stammer. She saves me. "I live in the city in a decent condo. It's not a place for crutches and my mom insisted that I stay with them. It hasn't been too bad. Like I said, it's a lot closer to the practice rink up the street."

"Is that where the whole team practices?" I don't remember it being grandiose enough for a professional National Women's Hockey League team.

She shakes her head at me and laughs. "How do you not know a single thing about hockey? You're the only lesbian on Earth, all of Earth, who doesn't."

I laugh. "It's just not my thing. I'll tell you what. When I think you're ready for skating, we can have our PT session at the mysterious rink up the street from the orchard."

"It's just a local rink. I just go there for extra practice time. The team practices on the same rink we play on, Bushnell Arena, which is downtown. Also within walking distance of my place." Hockey really is her life. "Wait, so if we have our session at the rink, does that mean I will get you on skates?"

I lean back and wave my hands at her. "Now, I didn't say that. I would just monitor you and your movements."

"So, you want to watch me?" My face is now the same color as my shirt, bright red. She's so flirty and for just a brief moment, I forget that she is my patient. A few seconds later, I realize this dalliance isn't acceptable.

"You know, watch your leg and ankle, make sure you are strong enough for your weight again and see how you move on ice. That won't happen for at least another week or two, so don't get any ideas." I wisely ignore her innuendo. I pretend to be really interested in something ahead of us on the trail instead. I think she realizes she crossed the line because she slips back into apple orchard tour guide. It's getting dark out.

"Let's swing by the store and get you some apples." We're quiet on the trip back to the barn. I patiently follow her to the front door. She is now down to one crutch and walking surprisingly well.

"Do you sometimes use your crutch as a hockey stick? Or do I even want to know this?"

"Only on the pets," she says. My jaw drops open and she laughs. "No, Doc. I'm just teasing. I love the pets here. Besides, the stick is completely different than a crutch. Although when I was a kid and I got mad, I would head out to the orchard and hit the apples on the ground with my hockey stick. Great anger management, and gave me a killer upper body workout." Her arms are incredible. Toned and sinewy. No, wait. I scold myself. It's just nice to see a woman in the shape Stone's in. Obviously, she takes care of herself. She probably hates carbs, too. "What kind of apples do you use to make pies?"

"I never really thought about it before. I usually just grab whatever's at the store and go home and bake pies," I say.

She rolls her eyes at me. "Would you like a recommendation?"

"Definitely. Tell me what you think is the best apple for the best pie." My stomach wobbles when she smiles at me. Her eyes are always intense even though her smile lessens the sharpness of her features. I have this incredible urge to reach up and smooth the concentrated wrinkle on her brow. I get why she is intimidating on the ice.

She limps over to the different bins of apples. I take a moment to look around. This is such an adorable place. The store is built like a barn. Every corner has a cute display with haystacks, pumpkins, and everything autumn related. There are still several people in the store even though the doors close in fifteen minutes. Stone greets a few customers and high fives a little boy who apparently recognizes her from hockey. When she breaks free from them, she crooks her finger at me and I make my way to her. "Okay, for the best apple pie, you should mix the Cortland, Northern Spy, and Jonagold apples. All should add something different to the pie."

"What about Red Delicious?" The disgusted look on her face makes me laugh. "Okay, apple-snob, what's wrong with them?"

"Nothing as long as you don't mind soggy, mushy pie. Red Delicious apples are for snacking on only. And that's only if you are six years old. Trust me." She grabs a cart and starts loading it up with entirely too many apples and I have to stop her.

"Hang on. I'm only going to make a pie or two," I say.

"It takes just as much work to make one pie as it does five or six." At least she stops adding apples to the cart.

"Peeling apples. Ugh." She smiles at me and pushes me over to the wall display where there are several different kinds of apple peelers from manual ones that promise to peel the apple in thirty seconds just by cranking the handle, to the automatic kind that will core and peel the apple in five seconds. "Wait. This is cheating.

Part of the whole process is sweating while peeling thirty pounds of apples over the kitchen sink, then spilling flour everywhere. The cleanup should take just as long as the prep work."

"Who are you? You sound like my grandma. I thought you were my age. Congrats, though, for being beautiful at eighty."

I smile and look away. She called me beautiful. I really need to leave the orchard because I'm starting to like being near her. I play it off. "Ha. Funny. I'm thirty-one and older than you so respect your elders." I always say stupid things when I'm nervous. She must sense that I'm uncomfortable because she grabs one of the automatic peelers and wheels my cart to the front of the store, steering the conversation back to apple pie.

"I expect a pie, Doc. There are plenty of apples in your cart. Thanks for the ride home." She tells the cashier to give me the family discount even though I protest.

"Stone, I can pay full price. You don't have to give me any type of discount." I feel like I'm taking advantage of her. She waves me off.

"It's okay. You're doing a lot for me, Hayley." She doesn't call me Doc so I know she's serious. "This is my way of thanking you."

I nod. "Well, I appreciate it and, even though I will be entirely self-conscious and nervous, I will bring you a pie."

She leans close to me and I gasp at her nearness. "I'm sure I will love it." She looks at my mouth for a few seconds, then makes eye contact with me. "See you tomorrow, Doc." I exhale, not even realizing I've been holding my breath. She backs away slowly, her eyes never leaving mine. "Brian, can you please help Hayley out?" And just like that, our moment is gone. She winks at me and leaves the store. What just happened?

Chapter Seven

I make two trips to the car to get all of the apples and other ingredients up to the condo. Thankfully, we have an elevator and a wheeled cart for such an event. We are on the tenth floor and I can't imagine having to haul thirty pounds of apples and flour up the stairs. Alison isn't home yet. It's seven fifteen. She usually gets home between eight and nine. Her late hours used to bother me, but now I actually enjoy the solitude most nights. I can move at my own pace and do what I want to do. I slip into comfortable clothes and tackle the apples. After fidgeting with the automatic peeler and finally getting it to work, I wonder how I ever manually peeled apples with a paring knife before. This is so much simpler and faster. I'm done with all of the apples in less than twenty minutes. I make up the recipe since I'm cooking with apples I'm not familiar with and pray everything tastes good. As long as the crusts are flaky and I douse them with enough sugar and cinnamon, the pies should taste great. I ignore the voice in the back of my head telling me to make the best pie ever for Stone. Not because I'm trying to impress her, but because it's the nice thing to do since she gave me a steep discount. I have to wait on the dough so I throw some forbidden pasta on the stove and grate parmesan cheese for a quick dinner.

"Something smells delish." Alison walks in and heads for the giant bowl of sliced apples on the counter.

"Don't touch that. I'm baking pies."

"What's the occasion?" She tosses her messenger bag on the table and grabs a bottled water from the refrigerator.

"I just felt like it. One of my patients owns an orchard and I wanted to pick up some cider and apples to make pies."

"A five-year-old owns an orchard?" I know she's teasing, but I haven't told her that a twenty-eight-year-old has been thrown my way.

"Well, Gloria gave me an adult patient who is recuperating from a fibula break and fractured ankle. Kind of a personal favor for her." I downplay it like it's no big deal even though my heart hammers inside of me. Guilt washes over me for no reason other than to serve as a reminder that I've had more than one lustful thought about Stone.

"What happened?" Here's where it gets tricky. I don't want Alison to know who it is. She has always been the jealous type. I don't see what good will come of me telling her that my newest patient is a beautiful, famous athlete who also happens to be a single lesbian.

"A dropped cell phone which led to a car wreck." I shrug to downplay it. I also don't mention pronouns. "Do you want to take a pie or two to work? I have enough here if you do." I deflect and hope she doesn't continue to press me.

"Sure. How many are you taking?"

"I'm taking three. You can take the rest, or we can dole them out to people we know," I say, thankful that she seems to be over my new patient.

"Jesus, how many are you making?" It's ridiculous that I went a little crazy on the apples, but I blame Stone. She was very adamant about what kind of apples I should use. "Why are you smiling?" Busted again.

"I did get a little crazy, huh? Oh, well. I'm sure it will be easy enough to get rid of..." I pause to guess on my count. "Six. Six pies." Alison shakes her head at me and heads into the living room to work. I don't even ask her if she's hungry. I know she probably grabbed a salad at the hospital's cafeteria. I fix a plate of pasta and gobble it down before I start rolling the dough out. Twenty minutes later, I have four pies in the oven baking with two waiting in the wings. I'm pleased with them. I just hope they firm up like Stone promises they will. I should be spending time with Alison since she leaves tomorrow afternoon for her Chicago trip, but I'm still kind of upset about the whole deal. When I unloaded the car earlier, I found the box of invitations that I have yet to mail. That has to be my priority tomorrow.

"I'm going in early so that I can get some stuff done." Alison heads over to me, pajamas already on, and kisses me softly on the lips. "Don't stay up too late." She puts her phone on the charger and heads back to the bedroom. I guess alone time isn't going to happen for us tonight.

❖

I place one of the pies in Elite's break room for the employees who want a slice. The second one is for Gloria. The third one I keep in my office. I'll give it to Stone when we're done with our session today. I tell myself that she gets the tastiest looking pie because of her apple snobbery, not because I'm trying to please her. I look at the clock and realize she's probably already waiting for me. Tomorrow is our last day in the pediatrics wing. Next week, we will try water therapy, which means we'll move to the main gymnasium where she will really be put to the test. I think she's having a lot of fun with the kids.

"Hi, Doc." Stone waves to me as I walk into the gym.

I can't help but smile as I walk over to her. "Hi, Stone. How are you feeling?" My eyes travel down her bare legs. I try to ignore her muscular thighs, but fail miserably. I can't even imagine the shape she is in when she is healthy. She's lost a lot of muscle mass, but she's still fit and gorgeous. Next week, when we get into the other gym, we will work on strengthening her thigh and calf muscles with grown-up size weights. I know she's chomping at the bit to push herself even harder, but, true to her word, she's done everything I asked her to do. She's ahead of schedule and I'll suggest getting on the ice late next week, assuming her progress remains steady.

"Good. I'm ready for more." Her smile is lopsided and I feel a flutter inside of me. When she winks at me, I can't help but laugh. I know she's just innocently flirting with me, but it still makes me feel good. Her trail of broken hearts must be at least a mile long.

"Let's get the massage out of the way, then stretch you. I've something special for later." I groan when she gives me that wicked little grin of hers.

"Oh, yeah, Doc? Why do I like the sound of that?" She cocks her head at me. Flutter again.

"Well, actually, I have a pie for you, but you might not want it after today's exercises." We both ignore the pie remark even though it's right there between us. We stretch her and I'm impressed again with her progress.

"What are you doing this weekend?" Stone asks.

"I'm headed to New York to see a play and eat really good food."

She gives me her genuine Stone smile. "That sounds like fun. I love New York. And I love the theatre. What play are you going to see?"

"You love the theatre?" I stop my massage and feel her body relax.

"Why does that shock you? Do you really think I'm just a dumb jock?" She leans up on her elbows to see me better.

"It doesn't shock me. I just don't know a lot about you yet. I know hockey is your life and your family owns an orchard." I resume the massage.

"You know, I did go to college and I've been known to attend a play or two. I even like museums and art and all that stuff. I do have other interests besides sports."

I hold my hands up in defeat. "I'm sorry. That's not fair of me. Okay, what do I know about Elizabeth Stone besides her love of hockey? I know she likes to cook and bake and that one day she will bake me the finest cookies known to man, woman, and child."

Stone laughs and lies back down. "Baking is very calming. You might not know this about me, but I can be pretty intense. I cook as a way to release my negativity."

"You must cook healthy because you are so fit. I like to cook with cream and real butter and I love carbs and I'm going to order anything I want this weekend regardless of the fat or calories," I say.

"I say eat whatever you want. Are you and Alison going to New York as kind of a pre-honeymoon?" I can't help but roll my eyes. Stone notices. "Or not."

"It's just me and my parents. Alison decided to go to a conference in Chicago instead." I want to tell her more, but it's personal. I have to stay professional, something I keep forgetting.

"What does Alison do for a living?"

"She's an orthopedic surgeon at Regional."

Stone nods her head. "That's great. Both of you are doctors. Makes for fun dinner conversation and probably gives you a lot to talk about. How did you two meet?" I tell her about the fund-raiser coming up and how we met at it when Regional Hospital was one of the sponsors. "Tell me more about the fund-raiser."

"We raise money to help grant wishes and dreams to the local Children's Dream Maker organization."

"Are all the children there terminal?" Stone's voice is low and serious.

"Most of them are, but some defy the odds and pull though." She smiles at that.

"Okay, finish your stretches. I'll be right back." Knowing how competitive Stone is, I'm going to end her session on a high note. I briefly talk to Matt and head over to the storage area. I walk back to Stone who thinks she is done for the day.

"Before you leave, I'm going to challenge you to a duel of sorts."

She laughs. "Whose heart are we fighting for, Doc? I'm pretty sure yours is taken."

• 49 •

That makes my body warm. "Cute, but not that kind of duel. You and Ethan are going to pick up marbles with your feet. Sounds easy, huh?" I wave Ethan and Matt over to the mat. Ethan, a bulky eleven-year-old football player, broke his ankle while riding his bike.

"Are you kidding?" she asks.

I wink at her and drop several marbles in front of her and Ethan. "First one to collect five wins. One, two, three, go!" Ethan grabs his first one with ease. Stone struggles to get her foot over the marble.

"No fair. He has long possum toes. Like hands. Is this even fair?" Ethan laughs at her comparison. "Are your parents humans or raccoons?" Stone finally grabs her first marble. She and Ethan are tied.

"Your feet are bigger," he says, grabbing his third marble. He showboats by lifting up his foot and showing Stone. I love that they are both smiling and working hard. Stone is having difficulty with this task, but this is her first time. It has to be frustrating. She starts to work up a sweat again. She ties him after only a few seconds.

"Stone, Ethan only has one more marble left," I say as he nabs the fourth one. Stone growls at both of us. Ethan laughs. "Ethan, Stone just tied you. This is it. Both of you have one more marble left. Who's going to win?" I watch as Stone looks at Ethan out of the corner of her eye. Her foot is over the marble. She is letting him win. I almost hug her until I remember that's not a good idea.

"I won! I won!" Ethan fist pumps the air, high-fiving all of us. He also shakes Stone's hand and congratulates her on a job well done. Nice manners. Stone acts sad, but nods her head when he tells her she did a good job. We watch him leave the room.

"That was really nice of you," I say.

"I don't know what you are talking about. And this?" She points to the marbles and leans closer to me to whisper. "This is fucking hard."

I laugh. "I noticed you worked up quite the sweat there." She wipes her brow.

"I sweat at everything I do. Ethan didn't even sweat at all."

"He has yet to hit puberty. Come on. Let's head to my office. I want to give you the pie." She wags her eyebrows at me. "Leave your brace off."

"That's what I'm talking about, Doc." I lift my eyebrow at her. "Pie," she says.

I shake my head at her and don't even slow down for her to catch up to me. "Hop up on the table." Stone sits down and leans her crutch against the wall. "I forgot to check your incision to see if it's healed enough for what I want to do next week." She jerks slightly when I run my fingertips over the incision. "Sorry. Are my hands cold?"

"No. It's the touch thing. It still feels really sensitive. So what's going on? I'm not getting it too wet during showers. I've been careful. Patting it dry, wrapping it well. All the right things."

"Some sensitivity is normal. There's nothing to worry about." I examine the incision. The cut is pink but slender. "Next week, I want to take you and another patient in the pool. Can you get here earlier on Monday and Tuesday so we can give it a try?"

"Sure. What should I wear?"

I feel my pulse quicken. I've seen her in shorts and a T-shirt and she looks great covered up. The thought of losing half of the material makes my mouth turn dry. I didn't think about seeing her in anything less. It's too late to rethink this. Besides, this is the best treatment option for her. "Just a one piece or practical two piece." I hand her the pie carrier and her face lights up.

"Oh, yum. Dinner," she says.

"Here, let me carry it for you." I reach for it again, but she stops me.

"No, I've got this, Doc. Thank you so much. I'll give you a full report next week." I hold the side door open for her and watch as she carefully hobbles to her ride, the pie clutched close. Now I'm nervous. I tasted one of the pies last night and loved everything about it. I hope the one I gave her turns out to be just as fantastic.

Chapter Eight

I love the excitement of being in the big city. Alison is crazy to pick a convention over being in New York. My parents and I just had lunch at Alexander's. They are ready for a nap and I'm ready to shop. I'm going to have fun even without Alison. I'm pissed that I haven't heard from her. I know that she gets busy and forgets time when she's at a convention, but who doesn't call their fiancée when they land or reach their destination? I sent her a message when we got to the hotel. She told me to have fun. That was the last I heard from her.

I round the corner and plow into a woman. She grabs me to steady herself, which causes me to spill coffee all over myself. "I'm so sorry," I say. She looks at me, her blue eyes remind me of Stone's. She's tall, attractive, and I take a liking to her instantly.

"No, I'm the one who's sorry. I wasn't paying attention. Are you okay?"

I notice that we are still clutching one another. "I'm fine, thank you." I'm ignoring the warm liquid that is seeping into the sleeve of my shirt. Thankfully, my clothes are dark so the stain won't show. I pick up my cup that has now been crushed by a few people on the sidewalk.

"Crap. I made you spill your coffee. Here, at least let me buy you another one." Logically, I know she probably doesn't want me to take her up on her offer, or maybe she does, but I find myself nodding at her. "You got it next door, didn't you? Are you in a hurry? Do you have somewhere to be?" She is nice and I find myself smiling at her even though my sleeve is drenched.

"I'm just shopping this afternoon so I'm in no rush at all." She holds the door open for me and I take a deep breath as I enter the shop. I love the smell of fresh roasted coffee, more than the taste of it.

"I'm Rachel, by the way. Are you from here?"

I shake my head. "Hi, I'm Hayley. I wish I lived here, but no. I do try to get down as often as I can though. It's hard to beat this city's excitement," I say. I order a coffee with soy milk. She orders a mocha and we find a cute two person table open in the corner.

"I used to live in midtown, but now I live in Jersey. It's closer to my work," Rachel says.

I like to try and guess what people do for a living. She's wearing black pants, a black sweater, a wool hat, and a lightweight jacket. Her boots are fashionable and expensive, so she must have money. I decide she must be around my age and is in the medical field, probably a pharmaceutical representative. She is personable and friendly. She isn't in a rush like most New Yorkers.

"What do you do for a living, when you aren't running into tourists in New York City?"

She laughs at me. "Gah, I'm so sorry about that. I work for Pyramid Satellite Radio. I'm one of their advertising executives. They moved the business from Manhattan to Hoboken so I decided to move, too. It's amazing how much money I save in rent alone. What do you do when you aren't running into New Jerseyites?"

I was completely wrong about her. "I'm a pediatric physical therapist."

She smiles at me. "That must be a rewarding job," she says. It seems like she genuinely means it.

We spend the next two hours talking about our lives and I find myself having a great conversation with her. It's refreshing to talk to somebody about my life who isn't deeply embedded in it. It isn't until my phone dings that I realize so much time has passed and my parents are starting to worry about my safety.

"What are you doing tonight? Do you have plans?" I ask.

"I was just going to hang out in the city for a bit, shop, and then go home."

"I've an extra ticket to the play, if you are interested in going." She already knows I have a fiancée so she knows it's not a date.

"Really? Are you sure? I mean, isn't this kind of your weekend with your parents?"

"No, I welcome the company. As my new friend, just say yes." She really is adorable. We have already become fast friends.

"Okay, sure. That would be great, as long as you are okay with me tagging along." I shoot my parents a text that I've got somebody joining us this evening and we agree to meet in the hotel lobby. They keep Rachel entertained while I get cleaned up for the play. I rush for no reason and am back in the lobby within fifteen minutes. They are deep in conversation about radio as my father was a disc jockey in college. Even my mom seems taken with her.

"Have we decided on a place to eat?" I sit on the couch next to Rachel.

"Well, I was just telling your parents about a little Italian restaurant within walking distance of the theatre. I know the owners and they have reserved us a table if you're interested."

"Of course. I love Italian food. Pasta and bread." My phone buzzes and it's a message from Alison.

Have fun tonight. Miss you all.

I'm quick to answer. *We will. How was your day?* I wait for her response, but she is quiet. I want to know if she is thinking about me, or if she had a good day, or how her speech went. I follow up with a final message that also goes unanswered. *Sleep well. Call me tomorrow if you can.*

❖

"Do you want to go out for a bit?" Rachel asks. The play is over and we stand around waiting for a cab. I know my parents want to get back to the hotel. They bow out immediately.

"Have fun, girls. Be careful and we'll see you tomorrow at breakfast, Hayley." They kiss and hug me goodbye.

"What do you have in mind?" I turn to Rachel, the excitement of the city coursing through me.

"Well, do you want live music, or do you want to go dancing, go to a bar? The possibilities are endless," she says.

"How about I leave it up to you." I'm in my favorite city. Unsupervised. I watch her while she thinks about how she's going to entertain us. When her face lights up with an idea, I smile along with her. She could take me to an abandoned warehouse where they kidnap women and sell them. I'm completely trusting a stranger and I'm not worried in the least.

"I have an idea." She grabs my hand and waves down a taxi. "We're going to do all of those things." I like that she is holding my hand still. She drops it to open the door when the cab pulls up. "The C on Tenth and Bleecker. Let's make this a night you won't forget, okay?" When the cab turns down an alley, I get a little nervous until I see a door with the letter 'C' above it. There are several women hanging around the door, smoking and laughing. "Don't be afraid. This is the back entrance. The front is far more civilized." I wipe pretend sweat from my brow. She squeezes my arm. "Ready?" She pays for the cab, citing her treat, and pushes me toward the door. I can feel the bass and immediately feel my inhibitions leave. The large, muscular bouncer sitting at the entrance takes her money and lets us pass. She clutches my hand and drags me past two dance floors, three bars, and into a quieter section where we can actually hear one another. A waitress finds us immediately.

"Rachel. Haven't seen you in months. What can I get you to drink?" she asks.

Rachel turns to me, her eyes bright and devilish. "What's your poison, bachelorette for another few weeks?"

I throw my head back and laugh. "Are you throwing me a bachelorette party?"

She nods and winks. "A party for two. Maybe more if we play our cards right."

"Are you going to take care of me if I get out of control?" She lifts her eyebrow at me. "Let me rephrase that. Will you hold my hair back if I get sick in the bathroom?"

She laughs. "Of course. Tonight will be about you. Do you want to start off with shots?" At my nod, she orders two Fireballs. When they arrive, she hands me one. The sharp smell of cinnamon makes my mouth water. "Here's to new friends and fun Saturday nights."

"I'll drink to that," I say. She clinks her shot glass to mine and we both tip them back. She orders us round two. Oh, boy. "Wait. Shouldn't we be drinking and toasting my upcoming nuptials? I mean it is my impromptu bachelorette party and all."

"Fair enough. Here's to a life of nothing but love, desire, and passion. May you have all three every day with your lovely bride-to-be." Meh. I'll still drink to that. It sounds like a great plan even if Alison and I are struggling with two out of the three.

I stop Rachel after the third shot. "Let's just slow it down a bit." I'm starting to feel wobbly. "Want to dance?" That probably won't help my legs, but what the hell. Now that it's well after midnight, the club picks up and the dance floor is packed. In thirty minutes, an all-girl band is taking the stage, but until then, the DJ is playing great dance music. Rachel leaves for a moment and returns without her hat and sweater. Her black camisole leaves very little to the imagination.

"I was getting hot." She hands me a fresh drink and fans herself with her hand. Letting lose with Rachel is exactly what I need. I'm flirty and dangerous. Women are everywhere and we're dancing and grinding. Rachel's a great dance partner. She fits me well. When the band takes the stage, the crowd goes wild. I don't know this band at all, but the energy from the music and the crowd of women is off the chart. I miss being a part of something like this even for a few hours. Not that I break out like this all of the time, but it's just a side of myself that I miss. When the night finally comes to an end, I feel rejuvenated. Unstoppable. Alive. Rachel and I grab our stuff and head out.

"This has been one of the best nights of my life. Thank you for taking me out for my only bachelorette party," I say.

Rachel leans forward and kisses me right on the lips. It's a hard, full of life kiss, not a passionate one. "Hayley, you and I are going to be great friends. Thank you for hanging with me tonight." She flags me down a cab and helps me inside. "You're fantastic and don't ever forget it." She closes the door and disappears into the crowd. When I crawl into my hotel bed, a cheesy smile is still plastered on my face.

Chapter Nine

Stone's at the pool already, waiting on me and Brittney, my eight-year-old patient who had the cast removed from her arm last week. Stone is in a chair reading something on her phone. I take a moment to study her. Her brace, substantially smaller than the one from last week, is still on. She's wearing blue board shorts and a T-shirt and I'm disappointed at the amount of clothes she is wearing. She looks up at us and smiles.

"How was New York?" She puts her phone down and starts loosening the brace.

"What happened to your leg?" Brittney asks Stone. Kids. They don't care about interrupting people. It makes me smile.

"I was driving and I swerved to miss something in the road and hit a tree instead," she says. At her puzzled look, Stone simplifies her explanation. "I got in a car wreck."

"Can you walk?"

Stone looks up at me. "My doctor won't let me without this boot on, but I get to take it off to go swimming. That's why I'm here with you and Miss Hayley."

"Stone, why don't you do some stretches while I get Brittney in the water."

"No massage, Doc?"

"Maybe later." I turn back to Brittney when I realize how suggestive that sounds. I don't dare turn back around. Instead,

I help Brittney get undressed and into the water. Like Stone, I have shorts on, but I'm wearing a one-piece, purely professional swimsuit. When I turn around to get into the pool, I see Stone taking off her T-shirt to reveal a blue racerback bikini top that looks like a sports bra. Her board shorts are low on her hips and there is a hint of a tattoo peeking out by her hip bone. She is sexy as hell. Our eyes meet and neither of us looks away or smiles. When she bends over to remove her brace, I can see cleavage and I have to look away. Thankfully, Brittney is excited to swim and I have to keep my attention on her.

"Miss Hayley, can I let go of the side of the pool yet?" We're in the shallow end and Brittney is holding onto the side of the pool, kicking her feet behind her. This exercise will strengthen her arm without it even feeling like she's in PT. I will myself to stay focused and turn my attention back to Brittney.

"I want you to kick ten more times with both feet behind you, okay?" She nods and starts counting as she kicks. Back in doctor mode, I motion for Stone to get into the swimming lane and swim laps. She slips into the pool in the deep end and starts moving effortlessly in the water. She's such an incredible athlete. Fast, sleek, and determined.

"Okay, Brittney. Are you a good swimmer?" I already know that she is, but I want her to be excited about swimming and show me how good she is.

"Watch me." She doggie paddles over and I catch her.

"Can you swim like Stone?" We turn and both watch Stone freestyle swim, her arms cutting the water with little effort, her legs splashing behind her. Brittney nods and swims a few strokes but stops.

"That still hurts my arm."

"Okay. We won't do that again. Here, hold this under your tummy." I hand her a purple water noodle that she balances on. We practice a few different exercises including one where we slow motion sword fight with water noodles. She's working her entire arm, but only in a strengthening way.

"Stone. Hey, Stone. Come here," Brittney calls out. Stone swims over to us and I feel my breath hitch in my throat. I've never been this close to her with so few clothes on. She disappears beneath the surface to pop up right in front of Brittney. "You're silly."

"You're on fire today, Brittney. I saw how great you're swimming. Want to race?"

"That would be a no," I say. Both of them pout at me. "How about throwing around a beach ball instead. Stone, can you stand up on your foot instead of walking on your knees? I don't want your ankle to bend that way just yet." We are in the shallow end of the pool. When Stone stands, I watch the water pour down the front of her stomach and pull her shorts down even lower on her hips, exposing more of the tattoo. "Well, now that's not very fair. Stone might be too tall to play with us."

"I can just sit on the steps and move my ankle back and forth. There's good resistance in the water." It's like I've forgotten how to be a doctor. I nod, thankful that her body is covered by the water again. I can focus on why we are in the pool and not on her abs. We toss the ball around for a few minutes until Brittney's mom shows up. Once Brittney is gone, I focus my attention back on Stone.

"Are you getting tired?" I ask. We are the only ones in the pool.

"Not really. My body is humming again. I love that all of me is getting a workout. I've missed this."

"I think that's probably enough for today. Dry off and head for the locker room. I definitely want to make sure you get a massage after today's PT." I casually walk out of the pool and grab my towel to cover myself. I feel so exposed around Stone. While she gathers up her belongings and slips her brace back on, I head into the locker room and quickly change into dry clothes. She's sitting on the locker room examination table by the time I'm done.

"Do you want me to change? I think I'm getting the table all wet," she says.

"You don't have to unless you're uncomfortable. Here, put this towel underneath you." I hand her a fluffy white towel and she scoots it beneath her shorts after she removes her brace. I take a deep breath and start the massage. This time I hear a few moans escape. I press harder. This isn't supposed to feel good. This is just supposed to keep her loose. "So tell me the story about your tattoo." She opens her eyes and looks at me.

"You saw it, huh?" I nod. "A bunch of us were getting tattoos of creatures and animals that best resemble us and somebody said I should get a fire-breathing dragon because I'm such a beast out on the ice."

I laugh. "You're kidding, right? Please tell me you did it when you were very young."

"We were eighteen, so yes. My parents wanted to kill me. I like it though." She shrugs and lowers the side of her shorts to reveal most of the dragon. It's a cool tattoo, but instead of looking at the artwork like she wants me to, I focus on the sharpness of her pelvic bone and the curve of her waist instead. Hot.

I clear my throat. "It's definitely intricate."

"Do you have any tats, Doc?" She is still pulling down the side of her shorts and I swear she is moving them even lower. I finally look away and move back to her leg and ankle.

"No. I've always wanted one though. I just wouldn't know what to get," I say.

"Are you passionate about anything?" Stone asks. Our eyes meet again and I look away first. This massage needs to get over with quickly or I will never survive this closeness. I'm trying not to look at her nipples which are threatening to push through her tight, wet top. She apparently knows they are erect, but doesn't care. As a matter of fact, I think she evens brushes her hands over them. She's so good at being a tease. Not that I want anything else because I'll be married soon. Soon, but not soon enough.

"Not really. I don't have any hobbies."

"Come on, Hayley. There has to be something you enjoy." Her voice is low and smooth and her eyes are almost closed.

"Sadly, no. I work and don't play."

She's quiet for a bit. "You like the theatre. You like to bake. You like kids. Or how about something to do with your marriage? Maybe initials or interlocking rings."

"No. Alison doesn't like tattoos." I don't have to look at Stone to know she just rolled her eyes.

"What about you? It's your body. You can do what you want."

"I know." We are quiet for the rest of the massage. I end it early and Stone doesn't complain. "Are you going to change your clothes?"

"Nah. I'll be fine." She rubs the towel I gave her over her head and puts her T-shirt back on. She wraps her ankle and puts the brace on.

"Pretty soon you won't have to worry about a brace at all. You're healing nicely. Later this week, we will get you on the weights and try to build up your calf muscles."

"Good. I can't wait to get back out on the ice. I'm bored. It's driving me crazy. At least now I can drive. But going to practices just makes me want to get out on the ice faster."

"I know. Soon, Stone. Just a little bit longer. Go home and ice your ankle if it starts swelling. We'll do the same thing tomorrow," I say. She nods and slides off the bench.

"Doc? You never told me about New York. How was it?"

"It was the best time ever."

"Even without the fiancée?"

I nod. "I spent the weekend indulging myself."

"Good. I love that you made it about you. See you tomorrow, Doc." She slips off of the table and heads out of the locker room. For the first time since we got down here, I take a deep breath to steady myself. Being around Stone is getting harder and harder. Not only is she stirring the unfamiliar feeling of lust inside of me, but she is starting to get inside of my head. I'm starting to think about her as an available woman instead of a patient.

• 63 •

Chapter Ten

"What's going on, Hayley?" Alison and I are sitting in my car. We were supposed to go grocery shopping, but only made it as far as the car when Alison spotted the box of invitations that I never mailed out.

"I don't know." I can't look at her. My hands grip the steering wheel, my knuckles white and bloodless.

"Seriously. What the fuck is going on? Why are these invitations in your car and not mailed out?"

I have no answer for her. She gets out of the car and slams the door shut. I watch her walk inside and I know I should go after her. It's my responsibility to fix this. Instead, I put the car in reverse and drive away. Away from my condo, away from the pressures of this wedding. I need to think. I head to the neighborhood park even though it will be getting dark soon. Surrounding myself in nature always puts things into perspective for me. I find a weeping willow and sit underneath it. I make a mental list of everything I love about Alison. She's smart, ambitious, focused, and knows what she wants. She's attractive, fit, and cares about me. She's perfect on paper. So why am I so hesitant to commit myself to her? Why haven't I mailed out our invitations? What has changed in my life to make me rethink my decisions? I hate that Stone pops into my head. It's not her. It's everything else that has happened lately. My getaway weekend in New York was all about me and it was fantastic. I didn't have to check in or worry if somebody else was having a good time. I only had to think about myself. I felt so free and alive for the first time in years. I wore what I wanted and drank more than I should have, but when was the last time I did that? When was the last time I let go? I feel my phone buzz.

Are you coming home?

I look at the time. I've been sitting here for over two hours. How is that even possible? I wait. I don't know how to answer her. It doesn't feel like home.

I will be there soon.

I sigh and lean back against the tree. I know what I have to do, I just don't want to do it.

❖

I open the door quietly, a part of me hoping that Alison isn't waiting for me, but I know she is. She walks into the living room and sits on the couch. I sit in the chair across from her.

"Please tell me what's going on." She can't even look me in the eye.

"I love you, Alison. I really do. I love the idea of us, our life. It's just that even though I love you, I just don't think I'm in love with you anymore." I feel awful, but I need to get it out. I watch as the tears start falling down her cheeks. I feel them on mine as well. "This is the hardest thing I've ever had to say or do to another person. You are so beautiful inside and out. You will make somebody so very happy. I thought that was me, but now I just don't think so." She cries harder. So do I.

"When did you decide you no longer loved me?" She waves her hands at me when she sees my reaction. "Wait. When did you decide you were no longer in love with me?" I stand and start pacing.

"I honestly don't know. On paper and in life, we look fantastic. I just wish, with everything I am, that I felt it." I stop in front of her and kneel down, touching her knees. That makes her sob. She reaches out to me and we stay like that, holding one another, until the tears stop.

"Is there anything I can do or say to change your mind?" she asks. I shake my head. I lean back so we can see one another. "So this is it? No waiting, just cut it off?"

I hadn't thought that far. I didn't know it would happen this quickly. "I think that would be best."

"I'm going to lie down now. Can we talk about it later? I just need to shut it down for a bit." She gets up slowly and stiffly walks back to the bedroom, our bedroom, and shuts the door. I sigh. I turn off the lights, lock the door, and head into the guest bedroom. This is going to be a very long night and I doubt I will sleep. I sit on the edge of the bed and hold the decorative pillow that Alison picked out. I'm not tired. I'm just numb. I strip down to my bra and panties and crawl under the covers. I know I won't sleep, but I at least need to go through the motions.

Chapter Eleven

Well, this Alison I've never met. She's slamming things around in the kitchen, making enough noise to ensure that I hear her. I sigh and get out of bed. I head into our bedroom for clean clothes, a hot shower, and a moment to regroup. My eyes feel like sandpaper from crying and lack of sleep. I stand under the hot stream of water until I feel the temperature of the water cool. I dry off and slip into sweats and a sweatshirt, dreading the inevitable waiting for me in the other room.

"I'm glad one of us was able to sleep late," Alison says.

I stop from rolling my eyes. I also stop myself from correcting her. She's not going to believe anything I say right now so I stay quiet. I pour myself a cup of coffee and take a seat at the table. She sits across from me.

"I know this isn't easy, Alison. I didn't wake up one day and decide I wanted out of this relationship." I don't look at her, but down at my coffee cup instead.

"You could have thought about this before we decided to plan a wedding." She is brimming with anger and I don't blame her.

"I'm glad I thought about this before we got married. It would have been harder six months from now," I say.

"So I should thank you?"

I take a deep breath before I answer her. "No, you should be angry and upset with me like you are. I'm very sorry because

I know this is heartbreaking and it's going to be hard to tell everybody, but I think it is the right thing to do."

"You mean for you. This is the right thing to do for you." She stands and walks back into the kitchen.

"This is the right thing for us. You can't tell me you're happy with everything about us. I hate that your career comes first so often. I'm sure you get tired of hearing that. And you're constantly trying to change me and how I live my life." Last night, I thought this could be a clean break, but my anger is bubbling up and now it's going to get ugly.

"I don't know what you're talking about," she says.

"My identity with you isn't my own. It's not Dr. Hayley Sims. It's Dr. Alison Jansen's fiancée. We only hang out with your friends. You never show interest in my work because what you do is far more important than what I do." I wave my hands dramatically at her. "You change everything I do. I pick out furniture and you want something else. Our vacations are what you want. Even this wedding is all about you. I don't want to live in someone's shadow, Alison. I think I was just so excited to be with you that I forgot myself."

"I don't think it's been all bad. I mean, we have a nice home, nice stuff," she says.

I interrupt her. "Yeah, that you picked out. Don't you see? Don't you get it? I just don't want to spend the next fifty years being in somebody's shadow. I want my own life back and I know I'm not going to have it staying in this relationship." She's angry, but quiet so I know she's processing everything I've said.

"You're right. Everything you said is right. What if I promise to change? What if we start over and split all our decisions?" She sounds desperate. We both know I'm not going to change my mind and now I have to crush her again. I reach over and touch her hand.

"Alison, you will find somebody who'll worship you and want to be the perfect woman for you. I just don't think it's going to be me." She pulls her hand away and leans back in the chair. She looks horrible. I feel horrible.

"Well, then, what happens now? How do we tell people? What about your family?"

I hate that I'm taking away that relationship, but I have to stop trying to please everybody else around me. "I'll call my parents today and tell them. Please don't feel that this ends your relationship with them. They really do love you."

She scoffs. "Sure. That's great. Hey, Peg and Mark. How are you? I know Hayley has a new wife, but I wondered if you wanted to go to the lake this weekend? That just isn't going to fly."

I feel even worse. Alison has struggled trying to belong somewhere and finally found it with my family. Now I'm taking that away. "I can't make you be friends with them. I know they will want to know how you are doing. I'm sure they will want to talk to you." She starts crying again. Every tear I see rips my heart. She pulls back from the table.

"I'm taking a week off. I called my boss and requested emergency time off. I'll leave the condo and I want you to take what you want. I love this place so I really want to keep it. I'll buy you out," she says. I've always admired Alison's ability to adjust quickly. I should be happy that she isn't putting up more of a fight, but it still stings.

"This is your place, Alison. It always has been. You don't need to buy me out," I say.

"You've put a lot of money into this place, too," she says. I look around. It's all things she picked out. I don't want any of it. "I'm going to pack a bag. Just leave the keys when you're done." She stands up and stares at me for a long time. I can't even make eye contact. I stare down at my coffee cup. She sighs and disappears into what was once our bedroom. Turns out I have nowhere to go and less than a week to get there.

Chapter Twelve

"You did what?" I can practically hear Gloria's mouth drop over the phone.

"Yeah, I know. It's completely ridiculous and crazy and I don't know if I did the right thing, but I really need a few days off so that I can try to find a place to live and pack up some things. Alison is giving me a week."

"Holy shit, Hayley. Are you sure about this?"

"Yes. Truly. It's unfortunate that it took planning a wedding to see our flaws, but it's the best thing for me."

"Whatever you need. If you need more time, we can make that happen, too. Oh. Wait a minute. I know somebody who has a house she is trying to rent. It's about ten minutes from the office. Do you want her information?" Gloria knows everybody, I've decided. Sometimes she is too good to be true.

"Do I even want to know how you know so many people?" I already know the answer. Pete, her husband, is in politics. He knows everybody, therefore, she does, too.

"Just call her. I mean, unless you want to move into an apartment somewhere." I shudder at the possibility of living in a high-rise with twenty-somethings. My party days are over. I take down the woman's information and promise Gloria I'll be in touch with her over the next few days. She and Matt will handle my patients until then. I really do love my boss. I spend the next couple hours figuring out what I want to keep. Sadly, everything will probably fit in a small U-Haul truck. Most of the furniture will stay. I'll keep a few end tables, some dishes, two lamps, items from the linen closet and the pantry, and all of my clothes. In other words, I need to go furniture shopping at some point. With the Dream Maker's Fund-raiser coming up very soon, I really need to get my personal life in order so that I can concentrate on my professional one. At least that one is solid.

"Hi, Mrs. Dennis? My name is Hayley Sims. Gloria Bauer, my boss, said you might have a house for rent." I feel my heart race.

"Hi, Ms. Sims. Yes, my parents' house on thirty-fifth and Frye. They moved to Florida, but didn't want to sell their house. It's a two bedroom, plus an office, one and a half bath raised ranch with a single car garage. It's in a very quiet neighborhood. Would you like to see it?" We agree upon a time later in the afternoon. My head is spinning at how fast my life is changing. I have to sit down. I put my head down and take a few breaths. I need to talk to my parents. I'm not one hundred percent certain that Alison hasn't already called them. Another deep breath.

"Hey, Mom. How are you?"

"I'm good, sweetie. How are you?"

My heart is pounding. "Listen, I have something to tell you and Dad. Is he there with you?"

She puts me on speakerphone. "What's going on?"

I hear the concern in her voice already. "I just wanted to let you both know that Alison and I broke up." I cringe as I wait for their reaction.

"Oh no. What happened?" Mom asks.

"I realized that I was in the relationship more for her and less for me," I say. "I know Alison—"

"Did she do something to you?" My mother's voice is one octave higher than normal. She is not taking the news well.

"No, Mom. She's fine. She's a fantastic person, but she just isn't the right one for me and—"

"Did something happen? Did she find somebody else? Wait, did you find somebody else?" Now my mom is kind of pissing me off. This is hard enough without her interrupting me.

"Nothing happened other than I realized I kind of forgot about myself the last few years."

"Honey, we love you. We just want you to be happy," Dad says. At least he is rooting for me. "So this has nothing to do with that nice girl we met in New York?"

"Oh, no, not at all. Rachel is a good friend and I had a lot of fun with her. More fun than if Alison was there, truthfully. She just reminded me that there is more for me out there."

"Whatever you need. Do what your heart tells you to do. We will stand by you no matter what." At least my dad understands me.

"Thanks, Dad. I know this is hard for Alison, too. Please don't feel like you can't talk to her. If you want to stay in touch, I completely understand. She is a great person."

We talk for a few more minutes until my mother finally understands what I've been going through. By the time we hang up, they tell me they support me and my decision. It helps more than they will ever know. I feel a little bit lighter in the heart. I put on jeans and a sweatshirt and a little bit of makeup to cover up the dark circles under my eyes. I don't want to look like I'm an emotional wreck when I meet Mrs. Dennis.

❖

The house is in a nice neighborhood. It's a bit suburban for my tastes, but right now I can't be too picky. It's almost on the other side of town from where the condo is, so there is very little chance I will run into Alison. If we want to stay friendly, we need distance between us first. The rent isn't steep and it's close to the office. I sign a six month lease with the option to renew. My goal tomorrow will be acquiring furniture. I have a storage locker with an old dining room set and my grandfather's desk. That will fill up some of the void.

By the time I'm back at the condo, it's late. I sleep in the guest room again, only because the idea of sleeping in our bed makes me uncomfortable. I fall asleep almost immediately though, physically exhausted and emotionally drained.

Chapter Thirteen

"Your patients are so worried about you." Gloria invites me into her office and I slump down in a chair.

"Thank you for taking them while I was out Monday and Tuesday. Are things going well for the fund-raiser on Friday?"

"Don't worry about that. Let's talk about you. How are you?" She hands me a cup of tea. "Are you settled in the rental?"

"No. The furniture will be delivered Saturday. I have the condo to myself until the weekend so I'll just plan on staying there until after the fund-raiser."

"Have you heard from Alison since she disappeared?"

I shake my head. "I know I did the right thing. I'm sad, but deep down I know that Alison was meant for someone else and someone else was meant for me."

"You need to take care of you. Just don't do anything you'll regret. You know I'm behind you and support you," she says. I'm glad that even though she's my boss, she's also a friend. I need one right now.

"I'm just relieved that I made the decision before we actually got married." She reaches out and squeezes my hand reassuringly.

"Look, Gloria, I need another favor. This one you might not like."

She leans forward and rests her elbows on the desk. "Hit me," she says.

"I need you to take Stone."

"Is she the reason why you and Alison broke up?" Her voice is a little bit higher, judgier, and I'm immediately on guard.

"Absolutely not. I just need to step away from her. Honestly, I'm attracted to her and I know that's unprofessional. She's been nothing but the exemplary patient. She works hard and does everything I tell her to do without bitching. She will be zero problem for you for the next few weeks until she is done."

"I have to say, this surprises me, but I will gladly take her." She sighs and leans back in her chair. "She's been worried about you. She tries to play tough girl, but I know she's concerned."

My heart starts pounding and I wonder what she said about me. I try to play it off, but I still want answers. "What did she say? Anything specific? I mean, I feel bad and I don't want Stone to think I'm blowing her off." I try to relax my voice because I know I sound too eager.

"She asked if you're okay and if you need anything from her, from us. She's an adult. She understands things better than the kids. I just told her you are going through some personal stuff right now. She hasn't pushed for more."

I don't want it to, but it stings. I wanted more of a response than a shoulder shrug from Stone. Does she even care? Have I been reading too much into our exchanges? I need to take a step back and clear my head.

"Thank you for this." I stand up and head back to my office. My first patient isn't due until nine and I still have to review the notes from the last few days. I feel drained. Emotionally beat up, but I also feel clean. Lighter than I was. By the time nine o'clock rolls around, I'm anxious to get back to my routine. My morning is fast paced and I almost forget to take a lunch, but Gloria orders the staff lunch and sits in my office with me to share a sandwich and chips. She probably thinks I don't know what she's doing. I'm thankful she's making me eat because honestly, I can't remember the last time I did.

My afternoon is speeding up and I'm antsy the closer it gets to three-thirty. Gloria gave me a new patient for my late afternoon slot since she is taking Stone. I'm actually excited about meeting Ava because she's an infant and so far, my work has been mainly elementary age children. Ava will allow me to put my specialty training to work. Since Stone is in the main gymnasium now, I won't run into her over here in one of the pediatrics therapy rooms. I actually jump out of my chair when Tina buzzes me to let me know the Sullivans are here with Ava. I take a deep breath because I'm wound too tight. I slip into professional therapist mode and welcome them to Elite. I'm itching to get my hands on this super cute baby. Born at two pounds, eight ounces, Ava, at nine months, is behind the other infants her age in motor skills so I will observe her today and work up a plan to increase muscle tone based on what I see.

"Come here, baby girl." I hold my hands out to her. She isn't interested in me and starts crying immediately. "I know exactly how you feel." I take her anyway and hold her close until she gets comfortable. Thankfully, there are tons of bright colors in this room that are designed to get attention and she stops crying. Our thirty minutes are over in no time and I give her parents a list of things to try with her at home.

Parents generally react one of two ways. They are either eternally grateful to you, or they like to place blame. Most of Elite's patients are thankful for the therapy and understand that it takes time. We've only had a few parents and patients who struggle with not being healed after one or two visits. This is why I got out of sports therapy. Athletes are worse than babies, although Stone has been very agreeable. I should check on her. I say goodbye to Ava and her parents and make my way to the big workout room. I don't go in, but I watch from the observatory window above the gym. I smile when I see Stone. Gloria has her on leg weights and I know Stone is giving it her all. She's adding extra reps to her sets when Gloria isn't paying attention. I don't blame her. She's been good for so long. As soon as she is strong enough, I think Gloria should put her out on the ice.

I purposely leave early so I won't have to face Stone. It's completely childish, but I need to make a clean break from her.

She did leave a voice mail on my work phone about how much she enjoyed the apple pie. I never gave her my personal cell number. I always give my number to new patients, but now I'm thankful I didn't give it to her. Stone is a very determined woman. I have a feeling that she's not happy at being passed off and is going to want to tell me about it. It's just a matter of time before she finds me. I'd rather it not be today.

I head to the condo to finish packing up. I have entirely too many boxes that will take me several trips. I want to make the transition as painless as possible, which means being discreet in getting boxes out of the condo. A few boxes here and there shouldn't draw too much attention. I make one trip down to the car without running into a single person. I only run into one neighbor on my second trip down who asks if I'm taking things to the thrift store. I smile at her. She's a huge gossip hound in the building. The sooner I'm out of here, the better.

I'm able to get all of my work, summer, and winter clothes in the car and head to the rental. The utilities are already on. I pull up to it and smile. It's really a cute house, close to absolutely nothing other than a school, a library, and a ton of families. I'm probably the only single person on my block. I put the boxes in the extra bedroom and plan to unpack them later. I did pick up a set of dishes and a coffee maker. Really, as long as I have clothes and coffee, I'm set. Tomorrow, I will do a change of address with the post office. No biggie. Starting over is hard. It is terrifying and, sadly, exciting.

Chapter Fourteen

"So far, so good," Gloria says to me. It's officially the start of the fund-raiser and everything is in full swing. The entire back parking lot is roped off to make room for the booths and games. At first, I was hurt that Gloria didn't give me more responsibilities, but now I'm grateful. I couldn't imagine being responsible for anything other than pouring juice and handing out waters right now. We have great weather tonight. I'm wearing a long skirt, boots, and a thin sweater. Once the sun disappears, the evening will turn cool, but now, the warmth feels great.

"Stone Orchard donated several jugs of cider that we can warm up when it gets cooler," Gloria says.

I turn to her. "Really? That's great. Their cider is fantastic." Gloria looks at me. "I picked up apples and some cider the other week. The apple pie I made you? Yeah, Stone's apples. Well, you know what I mean." I blush and she smiles at me. "It is truly platonic. I just don't want to make it uncomfortable."

"She's doing remarkably well. I don't regret putting the two of you together. You've been great for her and she has a lot of respect for you. I think this injury really scared her and put things into perspective. Hockey isn't going to last forever. Hopefully, this injury heals one hundred percent and she's able to play for a few more years."

"Thanks, Gloria. Okay, go mingle and gather up donations. I've got this table." I hand her a cup of pineapple juice, which she sips and promptly hands back to me.

"This is missing something. Oh, I know. Rum." She walks off, shaking her head at me.

"I promise to add it after hours," I say. She gives me two thumbs up.

"Hey, Hayley. This is my boyfriend, Cole." Tina clings to a nice looking, albeit bored hipster guy holding a soft pretzel.

"Hi, Cole. Nice to meet you." I wrack my brain to see if Tina has ever mentioned him before. I draw a blank. "Can I get you anything non-alcoholic to drink?" I feel like I have to preface that for him or else there will be a drawn out back and forth about what adult beverage he can have here.

"Am I going to meet Alison tonight?" Tina looks so hopeful and excited.

"Well, actually we broke up last weekend."

Tina looks stunned. "Oh, no, Hayley. I'm so sorry. What happened?"

I wave her off like the last three years of my life didn't exist. "It just wasn't the right thing for either of us."

She hugs me because that's the kind of person she is. "If you think it was the best thing for you, then I believe you. If you need anything, please let me know, okay?"

I nod. I feel like I could cry, but I manage to keep it together. I hand both of them some punch to keep busy.

"Miss Hayley. Hi." Alaina comes over and gives me a big hug. Saved by a child.

Desiree is right behind Alaina and we make small talk about the fund-raiser. Tina and Cole say goodbye and leave. I breathe a sigh of relief. I thought for sure the whole office knew by now.

Desiree shoos me away to get food at their booth while she and Alaina handle passing out the drinks. I gladly accept a plate of chicken fingers, fries, and slaw. Not healthy by any means, but scrumptious. Right now, I'm all about tasty. I head back to my table, but stop when I see Stone and two of her friends getting punch. She is laughing with Desiree about something and turns her head when she catches a glimpse of me. I freeze. I hear her stutter for a second, then she turns her attention back to her friends. I have no choice but to head her way.

"Doc. Good to see you again." To the untrained eye, she's cordial and friendly, but her smile doesn't reach her eyes. I know she's mad at me. Her body language is brimming with anger.

"Stone. Looks like you're getting around quite well." I resume my spot behind the table.

"Yeah, Gloria has been great to work with." She stresses Gloria's name. Ouch. That hurt, but completely understandable. She's upset. I get it.

"She really is." Our conversation is strained. "You look good. I see you're in your final brace." Stone is wearing jeans with just enough of a flare to cover the brace. Her shirt is untucked and fitted. The first two buttons are open, revealing a smooth neck. I smile.

"I am. Listening to your physical therapist pays off." Stone looks down at the smaller brace. "Meet Kensie and Emily. They are Gray Wolves, too. This is Hayley. She was my first therapist." The girls are friendly. I'm sure they don't feel the tension between us.

"So you're going to get Stone ready for the season, huh?" Emily asks.

"Well, Elite is. I started her and the owner of Elite is going to finish. Stone's going to be back on the ice in no time," I say.

"We need her. Practice has already started and the whole team is off. We need our captain," Kensie says. Emily nods. These girls idolize Stone.

"Stop. I'll be back at practice sooner than you think," Stone says. "Then you'll wish that I was back at PT instead of chasing the both of you out on the rink."

As enjoyable as it is to see Stone with her teammates, I have to get back to serving. There is now a line forming. "It's nice to see you again. Don't push yourself too hard, okay?"

She does the head nod thing to me and walks away. Cold. I push her out of my mind and get back to playing drink hostess. Her presence here is in the forefront of my mind though. I know where she is, who she talks to, and even what she eats.

"Hey, I'm here to relieve you. Go have fun. Hang out with your patients," Matt says.

I've been at the table for two hours and I'm bored. Most people are done eating and they've hit the cotton candy and candied apple stage of the evening. Only a few new people are trickling in. We usually shut down by ten and spend about an additional hour cleaning up. Unfortunately, I won't be able to sleep in. My furniture is arriving sometime between eight and ten tomorrow. Then, I have one final trip to the condo and then I'm done. That part of my life will be officially over. I hope Alison stays away until Sunday because I really don't want to run into her.

"Hayley, can I talk to you for a minute?" Stone is suddenly by my side. I shiver. My guard is down and I nod. "Is there anywhere we can go?" This is a mistake.

"We can go inside if you want," I say. The clinic is open for the bathrooms only. Everything else is locked down. Luckily, I have keys. I know I shouldn't do this. "Are you cold?"

"No. The air feels good." Stone's body is always warm. I can feel her body heat behind me as I unlock my office door. I automatically move to sit behind my desk, then change my mind and sit on the couch, next to Stone.

"What's going on?" I ask.

"Look, I'm sorry for being a jerk back there. I thought you dumped me as a patient because of something I did or said," she says.

Well, that's unexpected. "I'm the one who should be sorry. I should have explained that I was going to have to turn you over to another therapist."

"I heard about what happened with Alison. I'm really sorry. I had no idea you were going through so much." A very sincere

Stone is also a dangerous one. Those blue eyes bore right through me. I look away.

"It's something I had to do for myself. I know I waited too long, but I just couldn't go through with it. Alison found the invitations in the back of my car. I never mailed them out, so it's not as if it was going to happen anyway." Stone looks stunned, but quickly masks it.

"I don't know you that well, but you never seemed really excited about the wedding. I think you did the right thing. With so much going on in your personal life, I understand why you had to release some of your patients. I just wish it wasn't me," she says.

I don't correct her. It's better that she doesn't know the real reason. "Thanks. I appreciate it. How's Gloria doing?" Stone shrugs her shoulders.

"I just have to tell myself that she's going to do as good a job as you would," she says.

"Hey, she taught me everything I know. Or almost everything. She's really good. I trust her with you." I just don't trust myself with you, I silently add. Stone leans back against the couch. "Put your leg up on the table. You've probably been on it too long." She puts it up. "Do you want some ice?"

"Sure. If you have some around here," she says. I head to the examination room next door and find an ice pack in the freezer. I convince myself that this is all purely professional and I'm just helping out my former patient, but I can't help but think things are different between us. The angst is gone, her walls have been knocked down, and we're just two women hanging out on a Friday night, talking. I hand her the ice pack and sit back on the couch, this time a little bit closer to her. "Although, I have to say Gloria's deep tissue I'm-going-to-break-your-leg-again massages just don't pack the same punch that yours do."

I laugh. "Remember when you hated them? When you squeezed out a few tears?"

She reaches out and playfully smacks my hand. "Stop. I've only cried once around you. That was when I first met you and I didn't think I was going to play hockey again. Now I'm ready to get back on the ice. Or at least I think I am." I shake my head at her. "Or close to being ready." I nod.

"Crying isn't a sign of weakness, especially in therapy. It's a sign of strength. I'm not just saying that. I've seen a ton of tears in my life. From athletes twice your size, and from children half your size. I'm just happy to be part of it all."

"Do you work with the kids from The Dream Maker organization? Because that has to be the hardest thing ever. I can't even imagine," she says.

"I did when I was getting certified. And yes, it was heartbreaking. Nobody likes to see children hurt, especially if you know there is a very little chance they will survive. Elite is geared more toward children who don't have critical injuries or illnesses." I lean back on the couch, too, and put my feet up on the table next to Stone's. "So even though they are hurt when they arrive, there's a one hundred percent chance that they will leave in better condition."

"And all I do is play hockey," Stone says.

"Stop. Don't even compare. We both have different lives. Think of how many kids love you. You're a hero to so many young and old athletes. We both do good things for kids. Plus, according to you and every other lesbian on Earth, hockey is the coolest thing ever." We both laugh at that.

"So will you come to one of my games when I'm all healed up?" she asks. I already know that I will, whether she knows it or not. I nod. "Actually, I'd like to bring the kids, the ones I've been sharing PT time with, to the rink. For a practice and maybe a game. I mean, if they are into it."

I smile. "That's great. The kids would really like it. You have a great heart, Stone, even though you pretend to be so tough."

Her smile couldn't be any bigger. "Now, don't go giving my secret away. I have a reputation to protect." I roll my eyes at her. She reaches out and holds my hand. "Seriously, thank you for all that you've done." I feel my stomach quiver. Her touch is so warm and soft.

"Stone. Please." She continues to hold my hand and softly run her thumb across the back of my knuckles. We sit there for a few minutes in silence, holding hands. I know this is wrong. I know this isn't supposed to happen. I should pull away from her, but I don't want to. Stone grounds me. She's gives me strength when I have none. I know it's because my world feels like it's crashing around me. Regretfully, I pull my hand away. Neither of us move or speak for several seconds. "We should go back out there." I break the silence and stand. "How's your ankle?" I lean over her to lift the ice pack when I feel her fingers on my sweater.

I look down, then at her. She is two inches from my face. I gasp at her nearness and moan when her lips touch mine. She isn't gentle when she kisses me. I feel her warm hand on the back of my head, holding me close to her while her lips claim mine possessively. Her tongue is warm and feels soft like velvet. I count to three and force myself to end the kiss. "No, Stone. We can't."

"Why not?" It's a question that even I have. She is still a patient of Elite. I can't make this personal. I need to stop this before it gets out of hand.

"We just...can't." I move away from her, away from her grasp, and head for the door. "Please don't make this any more difficult." She straightens her clothes and, when she is next to me, she lifts my chin up so that our eyes lock.

"We aren't done here." She looks down at my lips, then back up to my eyes. "We aren't even close to being done."

Chapter Fifteen

"She did what?" When Gloria called me into her office this afternoon, I thought it was because she was giving me a final count on donations. The turnout on Friday was great. Almost double what we had last year, and last year was the biggest yet.

"She discharged herself from Elite. Said she was good to go and appreciated all that we did for her the past several weeks." Gloria hands me the letter Stone wrote. I glance at it and tune Gloria out because I'm fuming. Stone isn't ready. She still needs at least a week of intense PT, especially this close to the end. "She promised she would do all of the exercises and stretches that she learned. She even said she was going to continue the water therapy because it made her feel in control again."

I shouldn't care so much, but I do. I can't let Gloria know that, so I play like it doesn't bother me. "Well, I think it's a mistake, but Stone is an adult and she can make up her own mind. She's very disciplined and I trust she will do the right thing." I'm angry at her. I want Stone to be better than she was before, but by quitting now, she risks learning bad habits and not giving her leg the right amount of rest. Gloria is gauging my reaction. I try to look nonplussed instead of angry.

"I think she might be back at her place now. She doesn't need her crutches anymore. I have to admit, her progress is remarkable. I made a mistake by telling her we were going to get her on the ice this week. She probably took that as the go-ahead to start playing hockey." She shakes her head.

"This is one of the reasons why I stopped treating athletes. They are stubborn and won't listen to reason," I say. It's not Gloria's fault. This is one hundred percent Stone's doing. "Don't take her actions to heart though. You did everything right."

"Her parents are going to kill me. I've known that girl for years," she says.

"Her parents know what she's like. Don't beat yourself up about it, okay? Hey, let's talk about something else. How did we do Friday? Did we raise a ton of money? I'm positive that we had a lot more traffic."

"A few people were going to mail in donations, but yes, we did very well. Twelve thousand more than last year at last count."

That floors me. "That's awesome. Truly." Our donations last year allowed several children to have their dreams come true. That's one of the things I love about Elite. Our involvement in the community. Now that I have a lot more time on my hands, I'll be able to participate in all of our fund-raising projects. We have one every quarter, but this one is the most successful.

"Okay, get back to work. I just wanted to tell you the news."

I leave her office still angry at Stone, but mostly angry at myself. If I hadn't allowed my emotions to get the best of me, Stone would still be in therapy healing instead of out there pushing her limits.

Chapter Sixteen

"What are you doing here?" Stone slowly skates over to me, her grace and confidence evident as she glides across the ice. She pushes a puck ahead of her; her control of it is truly amazing.

"I want to know why you discharged yourself from Elite. You're not ready for this yet, Stone." She skates along the edge of the rink, back in forth in front of me. I reach out and touch her forearm. She instantly stops.

"I think I'm ready," she says.

"It's good that you are on the ice practicing, but have you talked to Gloria about what your limits should be? Are you elevating and icing your ankle down after you skate?" Judging by the fact that she can't hold eye contact with me, I'm going to assume that's a no. "You shouldn't push yourself. I want you to heal as fast and completely as you do. You only have a week and a half left of therapy."

"I've got this. I've learned a lot. You told me to trust you, now I'm asking you to trust me."

"That's not fair. I've been keeping tabs on you. Gloria and I've talked about you and your progress. Even though she's extremely pleased with how far you've come, you still aren't one hundred percent."

"I'm not your responsibility anymore, Doc. You don't need to worry about me." I flinch and my anger is quick to surface.

"I do worry about you. You know I'm going through a lot emotionally. It wasn't my intent to turn you back over to Gloria, but my life kind of got in the way of this. I had to do what was right. That doesn't mean I suddenly don't care about you." I can feel my stomach starting to tremble. I know we are about to cross another line here.

"Are you this upset that I kissed you?" Her eyes are so sincere and vulnerable it's hard not to lean forward just to get closer to her.

"Yes. No. I don't know. I know that we shouldn't have done it," I say.

"It shouldn't be because I kissed you. Gloria was my therapist then. I know the rules." That makes me kind of smile. Stone sees the crack in my demeanor. She leans over the railing so that her face is only about a foot away from mine. "How about this. Agree to go on a date with me and I will agree to finish PT somewhere else." She is confident, in control, and so goddamn attractive that it's hard to say no. Logically, I'm not ready for a date, especially not one with Stone, my former patient. But my head can't ignore my physical reaction to her. My heart is pounding. I can hear it beating in my ears and I feel excitement course through me. The familiar throb of want resonates in my blood. I want her to kiss me again, even though I know how wrong it is. I want her to touch me.

"We can't." I feel the rush of hope leave my body and the heaviness of telling Stone no take its place.

"Yes, we can."

"I don't know if I'm ready to date just yet. I just broke up with my fiancée. I'm still working through a lot. I need time." She reaches out and cups my chin, pushing my face up to meet hers.

"Yes, we can." I pull out of her grip, gently, but firmly. "Come on, Hayley. Just dinner. Just say yes." I can't say no to her so I stand there without saying anything. "Let's just see where this goes. This weekend I'm traveling with the team for an exhibition game. I'll pick you up Sunday night. You have my number. Call me or text me directions to your new place." She glides away from me to the other end of the rink and disappears into the locker room.

I can't do it. I feel like Stone is my rebound girl, even though I'm the one who ended things with Alison. I circle around the ice and follow her into the locker room. It's quiet, but I can hear somebody rustling around.

"Stone? Are you in here?" I peek around the corner and follow the sounds to the end of the concrete room. I hear Stone humming and I find her standing in boy shorts and sports bra, her hockey gear already discarded on the bench in front of her. She turns to me, her body slick with sweat. I can't help but stare at her. She is chiseled and my body explodes with desire. I've seen her in less before. Maybe it's the fact that this is her territory and a different kind of sweat. By the time my eyes travel all the way up her body to meet her gaze, a wolfish grin is on her face. Oh, fuck. I'm in trouble and we both know it. I swallow. Hard. Twice.

"Hayley." She drops the towel she is holding and we both watch as it slides off of the bench and onto the floor. She takes a few steps toward me. I vow to stay strong. I exhale deeply and look up at her.

"I just came in here to tell you that I appreciate the offer, but I can't go out with you." I watch as she spreads her legs to straddle the bench. Those shorts leave nothing to the imagination and I can't take my eyes off of her. She leans down to take the wrap off of her leg, but says nothing to me. "I'm serious, Stone. I really can't." The doctor in me kicks in when I see her ankle. The redness and swelling is normal after her kind of injury, but I can tell that she pushed herself out there on the ice. "You need to elevate your leg and put ice on your ankle." I sit in front of her and tap my thighs for her to put her foot up on my lap.

I can't look at her because if I turn to face her, I will stare at the apex of her thighs and think about making her feel better another way. She knows she's attractive. She knows I'm nervous around her. She moans as I massage the tissue around her ankle, and my body heats up several degrees. She isn't making this easy for me. At Elite, she was very good at keeping her moans to a minimum. Today, every touch I administer brings out a little sound that is erotic. I can feel a trickle of sweat slide down the small of my back. I won't be able to do this much longer. I quickly glance at her out of the corner of my eye. Her mouth is slightly open, her eyes shut, and she licks her lips after every soft moan.

I move my hands up higher on her leg to work on the muscles, pleased at how toned she is even after the break. She scoots closer to me on the bench. She is already in my personal space, yet I want her closer. I hear my breathing hitch knowing that my hands are so close to her thighs. Her body is so warm. I don't even mind her sweat. Her thighs roll open as she relaxes and she quietly drops her other foot to the floor. I grit my teeth and keep my eyes on her leg. My peripheral vision picks up the juncture of her thighs and for the briefest moment, I picture myself leaning forward and pressing my hand into her warm mound.

"You need…" My voice breaks and I stop talking. I clear my throat and start over. "You need to ice this. Do you have a machine around here? I'll get you some." I've never understood the definition of bedroom eyes before this moment, but the look she gives me is raw with need and I quickly stand, holding her ankle and gently placing it on the bench. I watch as she closes her eyes and leans all the way back. She takes three deep breaths before answering me.

"Over there. Near the office there is a station." She points somewhere to my left. I nod like I know where and quickly move away from her, putting much needed space between us. What the fuck am I doing? I find an ice bag and fill it, taking a moment to allow the cold of the ice machine to cool me off. If this doesn't work, I can go out on the rink, strip down, and hope a giant block of ice will do the trick instead. I steady myself and head back to the bench. Stone is sitting up now, the magic of the moment gone.

"Thanks, Doc." She takes the bag from me and puts it on her ankle.

I hate it when she uses that tone. I know that means all her walls are in place and she's back to being guarded. I should be happy and thankful that our heavily sexual moment is over, but I frown at the loss of it. What would have happened if I allowed my hands to wander up her thigh? I think, no, I know she would have let me slip inside of her. She spread her legs for me. That was my invitation and I walked away from it.

"Here. Put your ankle on this." I roll two towels to get her leg high enough to be effective. "Lie back. Is the bench too hard? Is there a mat or something softer?" Her incision is now an angry pink and her leg is chaffed. Her skate was rubbing against the tender, healing skin. "If you are going to be stupid and push yourself on the ice this hard, you need to protect this. Add padding or a gel insert inside your skate to protect your ankle and leg."

"I'm tough. It doesn't even hurt." She leans back on the hard bench and closes her eyes.

I take an extra second to look at her again. She is perfect. Hard and soft with all the right curves. She crosses her arms over her chest. Her nipples press tightly against her white sports bra, their dusky darkness visible underneath the spandex. I bite my lip in frustration. I'm trying to do the right thing here. I lean against the locker and take a deep breath to steady myself.

"I'm sorry," I say. Stone nods at me. Her eyes are still closed. "None of this makes sense to me. Please understand where I'm coming from. I think you're a wonderful woman. And if our circumstances were different, then maybe we could pursue something here."

"It's okay, Hayley. I understand. I'm not your type." She sits up and readjusts her ice pack.

I should walk away. Right now. I should turn around and pretend the last fifteen minutes didn't happen. Then I could go home, take a hot bath, touch myself, and maybe even cry myself to sleep. Yes, I should leave right now. Instead, I turn to face her. "That's not true. I feel like I wouldn't give this relationship a chance if we tried it now. You need to focus on you and getting strong again because your season starts soon, and I need to focus on myself and figuring out how to be single again." She looks at me and I almost gasp. Her hard stare is a mixture of anger and passion and power. I press harder against the locker.

"You won't even give us a chance?" Her voice is low and I almost miss what she says.

She stands up until she towers over me. Her breathing is short and raspy. Her body is entirely too close to mine. I look down because if I look up, we will kiss again. I press my palms flat against the metal locker behind me and close my eyes so that I'm not tempted by her perfection. Her sweat smells clean and I want to run my hands over her hard abs and kiss the valley between her breasts. I want to nuzzle the side of her neck and lick the wetness from the soft space behind her ear. My attraction to her is out of control. She touches me first. I press her hand against me to still her movements. I don't know if I stop her because I'm afraid of what will happen, or if I need to feel her touch against me.

"Come on. Tell me you don't want this," Stone says. I loosen my grip on her hand, but I don't brush it away. I want her to touch me. She doesn't hesitate. I feel her hand slide down from my waist and circle around to press against the small of my back. "Look at me."

I take a deep breath and look up at her. Her eyes move back and forth from my eyes to my lips. I lick my lips in anticipation, a signal to her that it's okay. She leans down and captures my mouth in a heated kiss. I submit. She pulls me flush against her so that every part of my body is against hers. I don't care that she's sweaty. I don't care that just a few minutes ago, I told her this couldn't happen. I slide my hands up her neck and dig my fingers into her hair. I can't get enough of her. I feel her moan against me, the vibration humming throughout her entire body. I know this is a mistake. Nothing good will come from this. Her hands move from my waist down to the sides of my thighs. Her fingertips dig into me as she slowly pulls up my skirt. I resist helping her because I don't want to stop touching her. Encouraged, she slides both hands underneath my skirt until she reaches my panties. I whimper when she doesn't hesitate, and moan when she pulls them down. This is happening fast and I don't care. I haven't felt passion like this ever. Her hands are warm and strong against my thighs. I open my eyes when she stills her movements. I move my hands from the back of her neck to cup her face.

"What's wrong?"

She leans forwards and kisses me softly. "I hear something." We stay frozen like that for a few seconds until I hear the noise, too. Fuck. Somebody is in the locker room with us. Stone breaks away from me quickly. I push my skirt back down with a mixture of fear and humiliation. She sits on the floor next to her towel and bag of ice and acts normal. I'm trying to catch my breath and slow my racing heart. I take a step away just as three of her teammates round the corner.

"Hey, Stone. What's going on?" Kensie asks. All three look at me, then her, then me again.

"You know, ice. Broken leg. The usual," she says. She stays on the floor and grabs the ice bag from the bench, settling in as if she meant to be down there on purpose. I'm impressed that she can sound so cavalier after what just happened, but kind of hurt, too. Like that didn't matter to her.

"You need to keep your ankle elevated and on ice tonight. Okay?" I say. I walk past the girls and nod to them. "Go to PT Monday." My adrenaline is keeping me upright and steady. I walk out of the locker room and pick up speed when I'm out of everyone's sight.

What did I just do? Guilt rushes over me, flooding me with shame. I've been single less than a month. I feel so horrible. That should have never happened. I should have never touched her. I should have never let her touch me. Her hands and mouth were so warm, and welcoming, and fierce. She consumed me. It was everything I needed and wanted, but just not right now. I start the car and carefully pull out of the parking lot. I'm halfway down the street when the worst possible question pops into my mind. Where the fuck are my panties?

Chapter Seventeen

I should get a pet. I'm seriously thinking about having one for the first time in my life. A cat. One of those fat, fluffy balls of fur that likes to sleep all of the time. My rental house is too big for one person and I want companionship. Not anything complex like a fiancée or a hockey player, but a tiny appreciative animal who only wants attention some of the time, and loves me for simple things like food, water, and a comfortable bed.

I'm doing that thing again where I don't sleep. In my mind, it's probably because I have a new bed and new mattress and I'm just trying to get used to it. In reality, I can't stop thinking about Stone and what happened Friday night. What is it about us and Friday nights? The week before, she kissed me, then last Friday, she did other incredible things to me. I want her to call me because I crave her, but I don't want her to call me because we shouldn't start anything. I should chalk it up to lust, but I can't stop thinking about her. A psychiatrist would have a field day with me right now. One minute I'm hot about her, the next cold.

Even though I'm the one who broke it off with Alison, my guilt is eating me up. Did I do the right thing by walking away from our relationship? Did I just get cold feet? That happens to a lot of people right before they get married. I sigh and make myself get out of bed. Sundays are for complete relaxation, but today, I have to unpack some boxes. Alison told me to take what I wanted, but I really don't want anything. I just want to start over. I want myself back. I got lost in Alison's shadow. My parents have just started to talk to me without bringing her up every few minutes. As upset as I am about our breakup, I feel like it hurt them more. That makes me feel even worse.

I head to the kitchen to make coffee. The living room is a disaster. Last night was a movie marathon of action films to keep my mind off the Gray Wolves' locker room and everything that happened there. It was also a night of binge eating so takeout cartons and junk food wrappers are strewn everywhere. My affair with food hit an all-time low. I gather up the evidence, toss it in the trash, and pretend all of the processed junk isn't sitting like a rock in my stomach. I shake my head at my own weaknesses. First Stone, then carbs.

I use my excess energy and break down boxes that I've stacked in the garage. Alison called last night. We were able to have a civilized conversation for about five minutes. I ended it before it got awkward or ugly. She still has a lot of anger toward me. I didn't want to tell her where I'm living because I need peace and I don't need her to stalk me there. She was pretty upset. She's tenacious when she doesn't get her way. Some of her TFFs have even tried calling me. I feel like a jerk for not taking their calls, but they aren't my friends and never tried to get to know me before the breakup.

My phone rings again. I'm almost afraid to answer it until I see that it's Rachel. "Hey, how are you?"

"Just checking in with you. How are you holding up?" I told Rachel about the breakup days after it happened. She's been very supportive. I feel like she and Gloria are my true friends.

"Okay. Just getting the house in order. It's still bare even though I just bought a shit ton of furniture and stuff." I look around and notice I don't have any artwork or anything on the walls. "I need art."

"Oh, you should come back to New York and we can shop at some of the galleries." There's excitement in her voice.

"I just spent a fortune on stuff I don't even know if I like yet. I'm going to have to cut back on my spending for a bit. But I would love to go back to the city. Maybe a Christmas trip," I say.

"Well, if you need a friend, I'm available any weekend."

I smile. I'm so happy I met Rachel. She's lighthearted and fun. "Thank you. I just might need one here soon. Let me get this place set up and then you can come for a visit. I have to warn you, though. My neighborhood is pretty boring. There isn't a lot to do around here."

We talk for over an hour and, when I hang up the phone, I'm smiling. It's nice to be wanted and have a close friend again. The friends I had before Alison faded away because they got tired of Alison's controlling ways. I'm still considering getting a cat though. I could use the companionship twenty-four hours a day, seven days a week. My phone dings. It's a message from the weekend answering service at Elite. I'm surprised they didn't call me instead.

Sorry to bother you, Dr. Sims, but one of your old patients, Elizabeth Stone, wants your personal number.

Stone's probably mad that I haven't texted her yet. I'm just so confused. I need time to get my relationship with Alison out of my system. It's only been a few weeks since we broke up. I'm just now starting to eat three meals a day again.

I have her #. I'll give her a call. Thanks.

I know I need to at least tell her I'm not going to go out with her tonight. It's the right thing to do.

Hi Stone. Doc here. I still don't think tonight is a great idea.

I gently place the phone down and wait. I wonder which Stone will respond. The angry, bitter one, or the seductive, sexy one. Several minutes go by before my phone chimes.

What's your address? She isn't going to take no for an answer. My stomach flutters. I shiver, remembering Friday. What she did to me in less than five minutes was so raw and exciting.

We can't.

Yes, we can. Don't worry so much. Let's just go out and have fun. Pick you up at 7. Early night, I promise.

Why does she have to make it so appealing? How am I going to resist her?

Come on, Doc. Don't make me beg. Because you know I will.

Damn it. I sigh. I type my address, then erase it. Then, type it again. I stare at it for a long time. I hit send and squeeze the phone tightly.

I'll see you in a few hours.

Holy fuck. I have no idea what to wear, where we are going, or what we are doing. I jump in the shower and even though I tell myself nothing is going to happen, I spend a great deal of time making sure I'm smooth in all of the right places. It's too early to get ready so I spend some time unboxing clothes. I turn on the television, hoping it will keep my mind off Stone and last Friday, but I'm hopeless. Locker rooms will never be the same. The fact that it was all spontaneous made it ten times hotter. My cheeks heat up thinking about how strong and passionate she was with me. I'm disappointed in myself for agreeing to this date so soon after Alison. Not upset enough to cancel with Stone, but just enough to come down from my previous high.

Chapter Eighteen

By the time I hear the doorbell, I'm a complete wreck. My entire wardrobe is on the floor in my room. I finally settled on a pair of nice jeans, boots, and a cashmere sweater. I curled my hair an hour ago, but it fell from trying on everything in my closet and from running around trying to look good without looking like I was trying. I take a deep breath and open the door.

"I was worried you wouldn't answer." Stone looks sexy and dangerous. Always. Thankfully, I'm not overdressed. She's also in jeans and a sweater. She's wearing hiking boots, the right one partially unlaced and loose.

"How's your leg?"

"It's fine, Doc. I promise. A little swollen, but my therapist once told me it's going to be swollen for at least six months." She flashes me the sexy smile that's only hers and I shake my head at her.

"Do you want to come in for a minute or do we need to leave?" I'm so nervous.

She reaches out and runs her hands up and down my arms. "I'll be on my best behavior, okay?" Her eyes are happy and relaxed. Her hands are warming my arms and I can't help but believe her. If this is her best behavior, I'm going to be in trouble when she misbehaves. "Let's go. You can show me your place another time. I'm sure you're still trying to get it organized."

"It's a total mess. Especially my bedroom," I say, then groan. "I mean, I'm still trying to organize my closets and it's a disaster." She walks me to the passenger side of her SUV and opens the door for me. "Thank you." I lean over and open her door after she closes mine. "Where are we going?"

"There's a tiny restaurant near my place. Excellent food and a quiet atmosphere. I think it's a great start for us."

"Stone, let's just take this day by day and not put too much into it. I still hate myself over being weak around you."

She reaches out and squeezes my hand. "You're not weak. You're strong around me. You're one of the strongest people I know." She doesn't know how hard it is to resist her, to resist my feelings for her. I'm holding so much of myself back. "Tell me how you found that house. Have you been looking?"

"No, Gloria knows the family. When I told her I needed time off to look for a place, she suggested it. It's cute, but wouldn't have been my first choice. I just needed to find something fast. I only signed a six month lease."

"I think it's great. Just quiet. I love living downtown. There's always something going on and always something to do. Your neighbors are probably going to hate you whenever you come home late or have your TV up too loud." She winks at me to let me know she's kidding. She might be right. I know nothing about my neighbors. It's just a matter of time before they come over to introduce themselves. I think both sides have kids and dogs, based on the toys in the yards and the barking I hear. Cats. They're the answer.

"Are you allergic to animals? Do you have any pets?" I ask.

"No. Why? Do you have pets?"

"I'm thinking about getting a cat. I want to have an idea of what I'm getting into before I rescue one. Or two." With a house that size, I should consider two.

"Cats are great. We have a few at the orchard. They're outside cats that hang out in the barns. Some cats love to be inside, curled up, and sleep all the time. Our cats never seem to sleep. They're always on the prowl," she says.

"I want the inside cat who wants to curl up and snuggle with me," I say.

"Then you better get a dog because you never know what you are going to get with a cat. Dogs are trainable. Cats have a mind of their own." She's serious about it.

"Maybe I should hold off then until I get settled and figure things out," I say.

She nods. "Or get a cat that's older and has already expelled most of its kitten energy."

"You strike me as a dog person. Like a Labrador Retriever person. Or maybe a Husky. Please don't tell me you have a pocket Chihuahua named Pip who is probably somewhere in the car right now." I glance around as if a tiny dog might pop out.

Stone laughs a deep throaty laugh. "You're right. I like big dogs. They're fun to play with. I'm afraid of little dogs. They like to get underfoot and if I step on one, I could inflict serious damage. I'm not a tiny person." That's true. She's all muscle.

"You're very graceful so I doubt you would squash an animal. Plus, you're not much taller than I am and I think I'm pretty quick on my feet."

"Doc, I've been on crutches, in different casts, and braces. How could you possibly know I'm graceful? I'm the klutziest person in the world right now." She pulls up to a tiny restaurant, parks, and turns to face me.

"Friday. On the ice. You make skating look smooth and easy. Watching you the other night was beautiful. You're very talented. It's going to be fun watching you in action during a game." I quickly add that last part about a game because otherwise it just sounds so wanton. I'm not a brazen person. My sex life gives vanilla a run for its money.

"Thank you. I really have missed it. Honestly, I didn't push myself. I just wanted to see how it felt to put skates on and if my leg and ankle would bend the way I need them to," she says. We exit the car and walk up the tiny cobblestone sidewalk to the front door.

· 105 ·

"Elizabeth! Where have you been? How is your leg?" A tiny Italian man greets Stone with open arms and she walks into his embrace.

"Frank, I'm sorry I haven't been around. I've been staying at the orchard. Nothing beats my mother's fussing. You know that."

"You will do anything for attention, won't you?" They laugh for a bit. "Now who is this beauty on your arm?"

Stone turns to introduce me. "This is Hayley Sims. She's the doctor who helped me get better."

Frank leans forward to kiss my cheek. "Thank you. Hockey is everything to this girl. She and my Sophie used to skate all the time together when they were little." He holds his hand at waist-level to show me how little they were.

"How is Sophie?" Stone asks.

"Very busy with the grandbaby. She's beautiful. I have a beautiful family." He walks us over to a small table in the back. "I'll be back with the wine. Sit, please." He pulls out the chair for me.

"Oh, my God. He's great. And how come he gets to call you Elizabeth?"

"I've known him since I was four. Sophie and I skated on the same team for ten years. Then she got interested in boys and hockey wasn't important anymore. Frank and his wife still came to our games in high school because they knew everyone on the team. They have always supported me so I support them the best way I can by allowing them to call me Elizabeth." She winks at me.

"You're supposed to dial back the charm. You promised," I say.

She straightens in her chair and stops smiling at me. "Yes, Doc. Would you like a recommendation?" she asks.

I smile. "Please. Tell me what you love most."

"Any diet restrictions? Allergic to anything?" she asks. I shake my head.

"Then I recommend their lasagna, meat or vegetarian. You can't go wrong with either." I smile at her.

She winks at me again and quickly purses her lips together to keep from smiling at me. "Go ahead and smile. I was teasing anyway." We order the lasagna and dig into the warm breadsticks Frank delivers to the table.

"Can I just say how nice it is to eat pasta and carbs?" I say, sighing as I take another bite of the freshly baked garlic breadstick. I almost moan with pleasure, but then I remember who I'm with and suppress it.

"I have to eat them."

"Poor you. Every woman wishes she had your problem." I smile so she knows I'm teasing.

"I burn so many calories every practice and every game. If I didn't eat as much as I do, I would wither away into nothing. Truth. I tried some high protein juice diet thing some of the other players were doing and dropped a ton of weight. That made me weaker on the ice," she said. I can't imagine her skinnier. She's perfect the way she is.

"I wish I had that problem," I say.

"You look great just the way you are." She's not smiling this time. She gives me the same look she gave me down in the locker room. I shiver and look away. She is too intense.

"Thanks." I was going to tell her the reason was Alison's insistence that we eat healthy food, but I don't. I'd rather not let Alison intrude on my evening. "I try to eat the right things, but sometimes I just want cheese and butter and everything that automatically finds its way to my hips. That's why I'm so happy we're here."

"You know that if you started tae kwon do again, you could eat everything you wanted and still be fit and trim. I could help you with a work out. Hell, you could even work out with me."

"Tempting, but I think I just need to get settled and see what happens. My life has been such a whirlwind this last month. I know, no excuses, but I feel like I'm free falling in a way and that probably doesn't even make sense."

Stone reaches across the table to hold my hands. "Look, I know I haven't made your life easy either. I wasn't understanding when you needed me to be. I should have been your friend." She leans back in her chair and takes a sip of her wine. "I want tonight to be a fresh start for us. Let's pretend you weren't my doctor and we're just two women who are out on a date. I think we can both relax if we just forget about the past."

I sigh. "Thank you, but I don't want to forget about our past. Without it, I wouldn't be here with you. Want to know the truth?" She nods. "I feel guilty for spending time with you. I feel like we have two strikes against us already. I broke up with my fiancée and we kissed while you were still a patient at Elite. I feel like we're racing. And the kicker is I don't want to stop."

Our food arrives so our conversation halts. Frank is animated and says he hopes I enjoy the food. He waits until I take my first bite. I nod the minute the cheesy noodles hit my tongue. After my approval, he finally leaves us alone.

"Hayley, I left Elite so that this, us, could happen. At least we could give it a chance. We both know that I'm attracted to you. Besides the obvious attraction, I genuinely like you as a person. You don't care who I am or what I do. Do you know how refreshing that is? Seriously. The first day you had no idea about me, did you?" I shake my head. "So many women want to go out with me only because of who I am. My name. My job. Not me. Not the real Elizabeth Stone. I know that's my fault. Sometimes that's just easier. I don't have to think. I'm tired of that life. I'd like to try to have something real and I'd like to try that with you." Those sapphire eyes are so vulnerable right now, I want to get up and kiss her. My stomach is quivering again.

I swallow and clear my throat. "I'd like that."

She nods at me. We continue our meal in silence even though my thoughts are loud. What happens now?

Chapter Nineteen

"I probably owe you hundreds of dollars by now, huh?" Gloria is back in my office digging around for the chocolate donut flavor coffee. I toss her a vanilla latte flavored one instead. We ran out of the other days ago.

"No worries. How's it going?" I ask. I know she's in here for a reason.

"I'm just checking in on you. Are you moved in okay? Need anything?" What she really wants to know is if I've heard from Alison.

"The house is cute. It's quiet and peaceful. And yes, Alison and I spoke on Saturday." Gloria lifts her eyebrows in mock surprise, holding her hand to her heart as if what I'm suggesting is preposterous. I wave her off. "The phone conversation was about five minutes. She's upset that I won't tell her my new address. I just don't think she needs to know." I'm sure I'll eventually tell her, but right now the wound is just beginning to scab over. I'm starting to feel strong again.

Last night was great. Stone stayed true to her word. We had a nice dinner and I was home by ten. She walked me to the door, said good night, and left. I was slightly disappointed that she didn't try to kiss me, but we both agreed to take it slow. It felt like a real date. I closed the door and giggled. I can't remember too many first dates and how I felt after them, but I went to bed with a smile on my face and our date playing on repeat in my mind.

"She called me." Gloria drops that bomb.

For a split second, I think she is talking about Stone, but then I realize she means Alison. "Who? Alison? Why? I mean, I'm sure I know, but what did she say?" I'm mad, and I'm trying to be understanding, but it's hard when your ex-fiancée starts calling your boss.

"Alison is concerned that there's someone else. She thinks breaking up was a mistake and just wanted to know if there is anything I could do to convince you to go back to her."

I put my forehead down on my desk and groan. "I'm sorry, Gloria. I really am. She should have never reached out to you." I finally lift my head up from my stack of folders.

"Don't worry about me. I can handle it. I just wanted to make sure you're one hundred percent with your decision." She patiently waits for my confirmation.

"Yes, I promise. I can already feel the difference in myself. I feel lighter, and as bad as this sounds, happier. Does that even make sense?" I get up and start pacing. "I do love Alison, but there is no future for us. I'll make sure she doesn't bother you again. I wonder if she's already reached out to other people here in the office." I can just see Tina crying with her over the phone even though she's never met her. I roll my eyes.

"I don't think she's called anybody else at Elite. She knows you and I work closely together. The only other person she might reach out to is Matt."

"I'll talk to him. We both have therapy at nine. Thanks for letting me know." She nods and grabs her cup of coffee.

"You do look happier, Hayley. It's nice to see you smile again." No way am I going to tell her it's because Stone and I went out last night. She will be the last person who finds out about that fledgling relationship.

❖

Whatcha doing?

I smile and send Stone a picture of my yogurt and apple slices. *Not as wonderful as the lasagna from last night. That was incredible. And, no, not one of your apples.* I throw in an unhappy face emoji at the end.

The next time I see you, I'll bring apples. Maybe you can make me another pie?

She's such a charmer. I understand why so many people want to be with her. I can't blame her for having a past. It must be difficult to form meaningful connections.

When will that be? I can't believe I just said that.

How does your week look? We have exhibition games this weekend, which I'm attending, but not playing in.

How's your leg doing? The doctor in me will always want to know how she's healing.

I had PT this a.m. The new doc thinks I should be ready to play in a few weeks.

I'm sad that I'm not the one healing her until the end, but I understand. She did what she did so that we would have a chance. *Are you skating today?*

I will but only for a bit. I have to wear a ton of padding. It's helped so thanks for the advice. I haven't pushed myself. I promise.

I trust you.

She is quiet so I figure she is on the ice. My lunch is over anyway. What a nice surprise.

Chapter Twenty

"You sound frustrated," Stone says.

"I'm trying to put together this bookshelf. It's worse than anything from Ikea."

"You want some help? I can bring over dinner if you haven't eaten yet."

An impromptu date. I start to panic. I look a mess. My hair is in a messy ponytail and I'm wearing yoga pants and a large T-shirt that says Raging Lesbian. I needed an encouraging wardrobe to tackle this project.

"Um. Sure. If you don't have other plans." I'm trying to figure out if I have enough time to shower and clean up. I already know our relationship has the potential to turn into hard, fast sex at the drop of my panties. Speaking of which, I don't even know how to ask her what happened to my panties from the locker room.

"How about Chinese?"

"Sounds yummy. Anything chicken is good."

"Great. I'll see you in half an hour." She hangs up and I make a fast break to the bathroom, stripping off my clothes all the way down the hall.

My shower is quick with minimal shaving required. I change into fresh yoga pants and a sleeveless T-shirt that makes me look casual, but super cute. I keep my hair up because I can't work on this project with my hair in my face. Thirty-two minutes later, there's a knock at my door. I do a quick check of myself and open the door. Stone's standing there looking dangerous and hot in her tight jeans and leather jacket. She holds up a giant brown bag with one hand and a bag of apples with the other.

"Did you just come by to bring me apples so that I would make you another pie?" I ask.

She smiles sheepishly at me. "My mom actually made me bring them. They loved your pie as well." She lifts up a bag of beautifully mixed apples. I laugh.

"Get in here." I shut the door behind her and try not to focus on her nearness. I take the apples and put them in the kitchen.

"Did you murder this bookcase? How is there so much stuff everywhere?" She turns to me in disbelief. "How is this even possible?"

"Right? I just emptied the box and a zillion pieces spilled out. Some assembly required means don't forget to hire an engineer," I say.

She takes off her jacket to reveal a long sleeved Gray Wolves Hockey T-shirt. Red, black, and silver are strong colors and they look good on her. "Should we get started?"

"How about we dig into this food before we dig into that hot mess?" I ask. She nods and follows me into the dining room.

"Your place looks great. I mean, not that I saw it before, but it looks nice. Spacious." She reaches for the fried rice and serves me, then her. Her thoughtfulness makes me smile. "I hope you like orange chicken. It's the most popular." I nod and she piles some on my plate. I pour us iced teas and wait for her to sit.

"My walls are too bare. I need art. My friend Rachel wants me to spend a weekend in New York and hit some of the galleries."

"Oh, she's the woman you took to the play, right?"

"She's really great. She's been a good friend to me the last few weeks."

"Just friends?" she asks. She's jealous. I find that I like that.

"Just friends, I promise. I think even you would like her," I say.

She frowns at me. "What is that supposed to mean?"

"I just mean that she's so likable. I think she's the kind of person who appeals to everyone. My parents liked her immediately." I dig into my food, suddenly very nervous for some reason.

"I see," Stone says. She sounds sad.

"Stone, please. She's just a friend. She's not who I want to get to know better." I reach out and touch her hand. She smiles and I see her relax. "Plus, I really need your help putting this shelf together." That gets her to laugh.

"You're the only person who can use me any way you want," she says.

I almost choke on my food. The look on her face tells me she means exactly what I think she does. Tonight might get interesting. I change the topic to our families. That's a lighter topic. Stone has a younger brother who's in college. He's also athletic, but his sport is basketball. At six foot seven, he's the perfect height for it.

"Was he just not interested in hockey?" I ask. We've moved from the dining room into the living room.

She turns and smirks at me. "He wasn't good enough," she says.

"It's probably hard to be in your shadow."

"I really tried to help him, but he just wasn't coordinated enough. Hockey is very quick and precise. He had a hard time making the stick a part of himself. Now basketball? He makes it look easy."

"Are you close with him?"

"Definitely. My whole family is close. What about you? Any siblings?" she asks.

"I'm an only child but I think I'm pretty close with my parents. We take trips together and still do a lot of family stuff."

"Do they live around here?"

"No, they are in Connecticut. Not too bad of a drive if I want to see them." It only takes me three hours by car. My parents are close enough if I need them, but far enough away so they can't just stop by.

"Why do you live here?" Stone asks.

"I got the job at Elite. I love it. I can't imagine living anywhere else at the moment."

"I know what you mean. I've bounced around on a few teams, but I'm grateful that I ended up here in my hometown. My life is here. My family, my friends. Hockey. It's all here," she says. Stone tells me her history and the ups and downs of being traded in the league. "I'll probably retire here with the Gray Wolves. I couldn't have asked for a better outcome."

"Where did you start your career?" I remember reading about it, but I can't recall.

"Up in Maine. Only for a year though. Then I was traded to New York. Now I'm here," she says.

"I love that there are more teams popping up along the East Coast and upper Midwest. That means the sport is growing," I say.

"It's great for coaching opportunities, too. I mean, hopefully I'll get to play one or two more seasons, then I'm going to have to come up with something else. Unless I want to peddle apples for a living." She shrugs her shoulders. "All right, enough stalling. Let's get this shelf built."

I sigh and get up from the couch. I was just getting comfortable, too. Stone gathers all the hardware, puts everything in organized piles, and reads over the instructions. She finds the first piece and asks me to hold it in place. She screws in the pieces, her body right below mine. My T-shirt flares out a bit from my waist so I can't see her face.

"I think I'm just going to stay down here," she says.

Since the piece is securely in place, I'm able to take a step back and see that she is looking up my shirt. My eyes widen in shock. "Stone!"

She laughs at my scolding. "Eh, it was nice while it lasted." She shrugs and moves to the other side of the bookshelf. "I'm going to need you to hold this one in place, too." I narrow my eyes at her and she holds her hands up. "I'll be good." She wiggles her brow up and down several times until I laugh. I move to the other side and hold the board in place. My shirt flares out again, but I leave it. Stone doesn't say anything. We manage to put the bookshelf together, quietly, and quickly. "I can't believe you couldn't put this together yourself. Easy peasy," Stone says.

"What about all of these pieces?" I point at the pile on the floor.

Stone reaches out and shakes the bookshelf. It's sturdy and doesn't give. "Strictly extras. I have no idea where they go and they're not on the directions. I say throw them in a box and move on. Where do you want this?" she asks.

"Oh, I can move it. Thanks, though." I'm nervous. I start chewing on my bottom lip.

"Come on. I'm here. Use me," she says.

"My bedroom," I say, not looking at her.

"Oh. Well, let's put a few pieces of cardboard underneath it and slide it back there." Her face is emotionless. I can feel my cheeks redden. "It will only take a minute." I nod. She slips cardboard under each corner. "Okay, lead the way." I pull while she pushes so I'm facing her. Her eyes are blazing tonight. I can tell she is turned on. I remember those eyes from the locker room.

"How's your ankle?" I don't like that she's pushing. That's a lot of stress on it.

"I'm fine. Really. The cardboard makes it easy."

"It's a great little trick. Thank you for doing this with me." She winks at me over the top of the bookshelf. My heart hiccups. We have to move the bookshelf in and out of the doorway several times before we finally get the right angle to slide it into the room. By the time it's in the place I want it, both of us have worked up a sweat.

"This is nice. Is everything new?" Stone looks around. Thankfully, my room is relatively clean. I even made the bed.

"Yes. I'm still getting used to the bed though," I say, then cringe.

"I like your bed. It's low. And big."

"I have no idea why I got a king, but I do like the space," I say. Stone nods and walks out of the room. I follow her, understanding the need to get out of there. "You're walking well."

"I feel good. It's still a little tight, but I can walk without limping now."

I don't realize how close I am to her, but I want to make sure she is okay. "Can I take a look at it?" I look up at her, her nearness affecting me more than I expect.

"Sure." She walks over to the couch and slips off her brace. It's tight, but she is able to take if off without too much difficulty. I sit down on the couch and have her put her leg on my lap. The incision has healed nicely and even though her ankle is swollen, it's nothing out of the ordinary. "See? I've been putting gel padding along the incision and taking care of my leg and my ankle. Nobody wants me to heal as much as I do." I move her ankle forward, back, side to side. Without even knowing it, I start a deep tissue massage. The worst thing for her is scar tissue and I don't know that I trust anybody else to do as good a job as I can. "I hate that I've missed this abuse, Doc. Nobody does this like you do."

"Sad that out of everything, this is what you miss most." I playfully pout.

"I miss your touch. You were always gentle with me." That makes me smile. "And you never put up with my crap. And you never knew who I was," she says.

I laugh at that memory. "I had to Google you because I had no idea. You're all over the Internet. Mostly good stuff."

She laughs. "Mostly good? Well, don't believe the bad. Most of it at least. I'm actually a pretty decent person."

"I know that. I think you have this big, bad hockey persona for your reputation, but you really are gentle as a kitten."

She sits up and moves closer to me. "You can never tell anybody that, okay?" I know she's joking, but this close to her, I'm having a hard time laughing. She is in my personal space and I only have to lean forward to kiss her again. She looks down at my lips. I watch her lips part slightly and her tongue dart out to wet them. Kissing her right now would be a mistake. She's so warm and by the look on her face, so willing. Her breathing becomes shallow. "It's getting late. I should probably go." She carefully removes her leg from my lap and puts the brace back on her ankle.

I'm very quiet. I want her to stay, but I know we aren't ready for that yet. She taps my knee before she stands. It's nine which is still early, but I understand her need to get away. I need her to get away, too.

"Thanks for dinner and for rescuing me tonight," I say.

"It was fun even if I had to work the whole time."

I put my hand on her arm. "I won't put you to work the next time you come over." She lifts her eyebrow and I look away. "Let me know your schedule and I'll cook for us."

"I'm free every night except Friday and Saturday. This weekend we're in town, but I won't get out of there until late."

"How about Thursday?"

"I would like that. Let me know if you want me to bring anything," she says. She runs her fingertips along my jaw and up to my mouth. She presses her fingers to her lips, then to mine. For something so simple, it's very erotic. "Good night, Hayley." She slips out of the door before I have a chance to respond.

"Good night, Stone," I say quietly. I shut the door and lean against it. How can one simple touch set my body on fire? I head for the bathroom to take a shower to cool off, but I end up touching myself under the hot stream and picture Stone's mouth on me instead. My orgasm is hard and I bend over from the force of it. My knees are wobbly and I'm breathless. Hopefully, this will hold me over until we decide to take our relationship to the next level, which could be as soon as Thursday.

Chapter Twenty-one

"I need to leave early today. As soon as I'm done with Ava. Are you okay with that?"

Gloria looks up from her pile of paperwork. "That's fine. What's going on?"

I'm not about to tell her I have a hot date with my former patient, the child of one of her friends. Nope. I'm not ready to tell her yet.

"I have to pick up a few things before stores close." I downplay it. She falls for it.

"That's fine. See you in the morning. Have a good night." She returns to her paperwork.

I shut the door and swallow a whoop of delight. I have to get to the grocery store and figure out what I'm going to make for dinner tonight. We both love Italian and chicken, but I want tonight's meal to be special, yet light. I'll start off with a salad with balsamic vinegar dressing. I decide on brown sugar spiced baked chicken with pesto brown rice pilaf. It's quick, but tastes like I spent hours on it. I did take all of my cookware from the condo so the only thing I need is the ingredients.

"Baby Ava is here," Tina announces through the intercom system. Already? I look at my watch. They're early, but that only helps me.

"Okay, I'll be right there." I fold my grocery list in half and slip it into my back pocket. At least I got my list made. "Come here, baby girl." Ava now comes to me without hesitation. I bounce her slightly on my hip as I take her into the therapy room, her parents in tow. "How has she been doing?" The Sullivans are very involved with getting Ava, their first baby, on track.

"We've been doing the exercises with her and I really think they're helping," Marti says. I can see improvement, too. I roll Ava over and work on tightening her tiny muscles in her legs and arms. She doesn't mind our little exercises. She loves the attention. Now that she is used to me, she's even more enthusiastic during our time together. That just means she wants to please me and her parents. She makes me want to have a child of my own. Wait. Where did that come from?

In no time at all, our session is over. As sad as I am to see her go, I'm anxious to get out of here and get my shopping done. I hand her back to her parents and say my goodbyes. Stone is going to be at my house in less than three hours and I still need to shop, cook, clean, and shower.

❖

"I brought white and red wines. I wasn't sure what to bring and you didn't answer your phone." Stone is at my door holding two bottles of wine.

"I'm so sorry. I've been busy since I got home. Please come in," I say. She follows me in and I offer to take her coat. She's wearing khakis and a thin black sweater. She looks dark, dangerous, and sexy as hell. Her hair is perfectly messed up and her eyes are bright and happy. "You look really nice."

"Thank you. You look beautiful as ever."

I blush because I'm not used to compliments. I took great pains to look good tonight. Not too good, but good enough. I'm wearing a simple black blouse with tailored slacks. My hair is down and wavy, like I had it up all day and just let it down. She doesn't need to know that I spent more time on my hair than on dinner. I take her coat and ask her to open the white wine. I hang her jacket in the hall closet. It smells spicy and sweet. I refrain from burying my nose in it.

"I found the bottler opener," Stone says from the kitchen. She holds it up so that I can see it. "Dinner smells incredible. What did you make us?"

"Hopefully, something you'll like. Are you hungry? It should be ready." She pours me a glass of wine. I shiver when our fingers brush as she hands me the glass. If she notices, she doesn't say anything.

"Tell me about your day." She leans her hip against the counter and gives me her undivided attention. I'm not used to such intensity. I've spent the last three years with somebody who talked to me without ever looking at me. This is new for me. It makes me feel nervous and like the most important person at the same time.

"It was good. I love working with babies and today was baby day," I say.

"How's Davis doing?" she asks.

"He's only in two days a week now. Kids are amazing. The worst things can happen to them, but they are the strongest people. That's why I love working with them."

"You're great with them. Truly." The timer dings, interrupting our conversation. I smile at her and move around her to get the food. She is right behind me as I take the dish out of the oven and place it on the stovetop. "Mmm. That smells great." Her nearness makes me jump. I feel her fingers barely touching the small of my back, but her heat penetrates my thin blouse and I shiver. Again. "And it looks even better than it smells." After bumping into her a second time, she finally gets the hint and takes a few steps back. "Is there anything I can do? I feel kind of useless right now."

"You are my date so no. Just sit down and look pretty." She rolls her eyes at me, but takes a seat. I carry over the chicken and rice. The salad is already at the table. Everything is set. I just need to sit down. I take a deep breath and slip into the chair. Stone takes a piece of chicken, adds rice to the plate and then hands me the

• 123 •

plate. I'm not used to this nicety. "Thank you." I wait until she fixes her own plate before I dig into the salad.

"What did you do today? How do you stay busy?" I'm genuinely interested in what she does. How does a person go from full steam to twenty percent?

"I skated for a bit, had PT, and then I worked with the coach on some plays that might work for the team. I've had a lot of time to study old games, different teams, try to come up with something that works with our strengths and weaknesses. She seems very interested in my ideas. That makes me feel good." She takes a bite of the chicken and moans. "This is spectacular, Hayley. I love it." She takes a bite of the rice pilaf and moans again. "This is my new favorite meal. Please tell me there is apple pie for dessert."

Shit. I forgot dessert. I shake my head. "Sadly, no. I ran out of time. Can we just pretend the pie I baked for you last time counts as dessert tonight?"

"I think that's more than fair. I'm not complaining. Really. That just means I can have seconds."

"Well, thank you for enjoying it. I have to say, it's hard to cook for one person. It's just easier to go out."

"This is why I live downtown. More bars than restaurants, but when I bought my place, I was twenty-five and alcohol was more important than food," she says.

"I somehow doubt that you partied that much." She raises her eyebrow at me. "Or maybe you did. It's nice to see you've grown out of that."

"I'll have an occasional glass of wine or a beer with the girls. We're all getting tired of that scene."

"It has to be flattering to some extent."

Stone shrugs. "It was at the beginning. Now I'm old and the younger and faster girls are getting all of the attention. Trust me, which I'm fine with. It's like I said before, I'm done with that. It would be nice to have something real for a change."

"Stop right there. If you're old, I'm ancient. Remember, I'm three years older than you are."

She laughs. "My body is twice your age. I'll be in a wheelchair by the time I'm fifty. I've had a ton of surgeries, my leg and ankle will always hurt now. I've broken fingers, ribs, and even my tailbone. Do you know how painful it is to break your tailbone? I was way more miserable than I am now. Of course, I was fourteen, but still. It was hard."

I cringe. That's a bad injury at any age. "I can definitely tell I'm thirty-one. I ache all over some days. I can't even imagine what my sixties will be like," I say.

We spend the next fifteen minutes comparing injuries. Stone wins, of course, but I've had a few injuries that are strong competitors. I was in a motorcycle accident and broke my wrist when I was in college. Okay, it wasn't a motorcycle, but a Vespa, and I was going fast. I also busted a few ribs when I slipped off of a diving board and hit the side of the pool. That injury still makes me shake my head in disbelief. My poor mother thought I was dying. I couldn't breathe right for a month.

"So what made you get into PT?" Stone asks. We are officially done with dinner and I motion for her to follow me into the living room. She fills up our wine glasses and we head to the couch to get more comfortable. She sits on one end and I sit on the other, but put my legs up on the couch, curled up underneath me. There's enough safe space between us, but we're still close.

"I've always wanted to help people. I knew I would go into the medical field, I just didn't know where. Physical therapy is about healing and being on the journey with your patients. Sounds corny, I know." It's the only way I can explain it.

"No, I completely understand. Plus, you get to build up such a great relationship with so many different people," Stone says.

"So tell me why you love hockey so much."

She leans back and sighs. "There's no greater feeling than flying around on the ice. It's about calculations and trying to guess what your opponent is going to do before she does it. It's about control and timing and knowing when to strike and when to settle down. I'm sure once I retire, I will end up as a coach somewhere."

"What is your degree in?" Most athletes go for a business degree. It's general enough. Almost every single college athlete I worked with was in the business field.

"Communications. The plan was that if and when hockey was no longer an option, I would get into journalism," she says.

"You're very good in front of the camera. Charming and self-assured." I realize that I've just confessed to stalking her online.

"Interesting that you know this." A cocky smile slips into place.

I shake my head at her. "I already told you that I Googled you after our first session. Your interviews were very good. The camera likes you and so do the reporters." I roll my eyes dramatically at her.

She laughs. "Stop it. I can't help it that I'm charming."

"This is true. You're very charming. Whatever you do outside of hockey, you will be successful at. I don't think you have to worry about a career. Jobs will come to you once you retire," I say.

"At twenty-eight, I'm one of the old ones on the team. Sad, huh? Then I had to go and get in a car wreck and blow my chances at two more years on the ice. I'll get this season in if I'm lucky." She looks sad.

I lean over and touch her hand. "You're doing so well. I know the regular season is just around the corner. You won't miss a lot. I promise you. You might not be one hundred percent at the start of the season, but by the playoffs, you will be. You need to give yourself time."

She threads her fingers with mine. "Well, I'm officially done with PT so now I just need to get comfortable on the ice again." She releases my hand. I miss her warmth already.

"Try not to pick up bad habits when you skate. You have to trust your bones and your muscles to work the way they're supposed to. Don't skate a different way because you're afraid you will reinjure your leg. Most athletes reinjure because they are trying to do the same thing a different way. Does that make sense?" Stone looks at me. Her blue eyes are so hopeful and trusting. I understand why women fall all over her.

"Do you want to come watch me tomorrow morning? I usually get to the rink by seven. Your first patient is when? Nine?"

I nod. "I think that's a great idea."

"I trust you the most." I take a sip of wine to steady myself. Having Stone in my living room looking sexy and hungry is a dangerous thing. I get up to expel the excess energy that has been gathering in my stomach since she reached for my hand.

If I'm being completely honest, I want her to fuck me right here on the couch. I want to know what it's like to be completely consumed by another person. To let myself go and trust her as much as she trusts me. I head to the kitchen for a glass of water and ask her if she wants one, too. She's standing right behind me. I jump.

"You're getting good at sneaking up on me. I would've brought you a glass. You didn't need to get up." I'm blabbering because Stone is in my personal space. She's so close to me and so serious. I know what's going to happen.

She runs her fingertips down my cheek and across my lips. Very slowly, very carefully, she kisses me. She's so gentle, I want to cry. I reach out to her and pull her close to me. I'm the one who deepens the kiss. She lifts me up on the counter and nudges my legs apart. I tell myself to slow down, but I don't want this to end. I move my hands up to cup her face and hold the back of her neck. I spread my legs further apart and push into her, moaning at our contact. Her hands find my waist and she holds me against her, pushing back into me. Our chemistry is undeniable. Just when I think we are going to fuck right here in my kitchen, she breaks our kiss and takes a small step back from me.

"I'm sorry. I shouldn't have done that." Her eyes are bright, her cheeks red, and her lips already swollen. She's beautiful and perfect. We're both breathing hard. I lean forward and kiss her again. She stops us again.

"Why are you stopping?" I can only imagine what this woman is capable of and I want her to do it again and again to me.

"It's getting late and I made a promise to you. To us."

I run my fingertips over her face. She grabs them and holds them against her lips. She takes a step back and helps me off of the counter. My legs are shaky. She holds my hand and walks us to the door.

"Wait. You need your jacket." I get her jacket from the hall closet and hand it to her. I know that if I asked, she would stay. I also know she wants to try having a real relationship and take it slow, regardless of our short history. She pulls me to her and places a soft kiss on my mouth. She pulls away when it starts getting passionate. I'm frustrated, but I understand.

"Hayley." I look up at her. She sighs and leans her forehead against mine. "I can't wait to taste you." She turns and walks out the door, leaving us both breathless. I smile because I know that when we do have sex, it's going to be so worth the wait.

Chapter Twenty-two

I had a hard time falling asleep last night. My body was on fire. I took a bath and touched myself several times, but every orgasm just made me want another and another. By the time I crawled into bed, I was frustrated and exhausted, but my mind kept me awake. I thought about the whole night and our conversation. When she sat me on the kitchen counter, I thought for sure we were going to have sex right there. I'd bet my life that our next date will be explosive.

I pour coffee into a travel mug and check the time. It's only six thirty. I feel like I've been up all night. I'm glad it's Friday and tonight I can go to sleep right when I get home. I don't want to leave right now because I will get to the rink too early and it will make me seem entirely too eager. It's bad enough I threw myself at Stone last night. I'm so embarrassed. Again. With fifteen minutes left to kill, I pull up a video of her in a game just so I can quickly study her moves on the ice. When the video ends, I grab my bag and head out, excited and nervous to see her again.

There are three cars in the parking lot. I recognize Stone's right away and expel a sigh of relief that I don't have to wait for her. I grab my jacket and head inside. The doors are unlocked and I slip in, wanting to watch Stone before she knows I'm here. She is skating slowly, her stance wide. She is testing her strength. She slows down and adjusts her skates. Enough time has passed since her surgery, but she's nervous about it and I'm not about to stop her from being careful. She grabs her stick and tosses a puck on the ice. Again, I'm impressed with her control of it. She isn't skating fast, just working on quick motions. She stops when she sees me and immediately skates over.

"Hi. Good morning." She leans over the railing and gives me a quick kiss on the lips. It makes me smile. I wasn't expecting that.

"How are you?"

"Tired, but good. How long have you been here?"

I reach out and straighten her collar for no other reason than to touch her. "Not long. A few minutes only. How does your ankle feel?" She smells sweet and spicy, a scent I've come to know as her.

"It doesn't feel too tight. I stretched for about thirty minutes this morning. I think I'm good. I'm ready to see what I can do," she says.

"Show me," I say. She skates off, slowly at first. I watch her lean to the left to test her weight and do the same for the right. She skates the length of the rink, jumping a few times, testing her ankle strength. I cringe every time. I know she needs to do this, but I don't want her to get hurt again. It sure is different when you're watching someone you care for more than just as a patient. When she reaches the far end, she turns and skates very fast back over to me. I actually gasp. She stops sharply right before the railing, tiny bits of ice spraying up in the air. I make myself slip into doctor mode. "How did that feel?"

She nods. "Not bad actually. My leg feels tight, but my ankle feels good. Of course, I've only been skating for thirty minutes or so and not very fast. I know I'm a week or two out from getting playing time."

"Are you okay with that?" I ask. There's only one more weekend of exhibition games and then the real season starts a week from tomorrow.

"You told me I'd be ready for the first game. I'm ready. Maybe not as a starter, but I could get away with a few minutes here and there." She smiles wide and, for the first time, I see a tiny dimple in her left cheek.

"So you feel like you're ready for this?"

She moves closer to me. "Definitely, Doc." My heart speeds up the closer her lips get to mine. "Thank you for dinner last night." I shiver remembering the last thing she said to me before she walked out of the door. It's incredible how well our lips fit together and how quickly our passion ignites.

"It was entirely my pleasure," I say, flirtatiously.

She takes a deep breath and pushes back from the railing. "I'm going to skate away right now because you, Dr. Hayley Sims, are dangerous."

That surprises me. She should know that she's the dangerous one. I shake my head at her. "Not even true. Go skate anyway. I want to watch you a little bit longer."

She flips into hockey player again and I spend the next thirty minutes watching her skate on one leg, then the other. She adjusts her skate several times so I know there is still some discomfort. As beautiful as she is on the ice, I'm more impressed with her ability to dribble the puck. Her gloves look so incredibly awkward and big, but she's so gentle with the stick. The puck is a blur every time she shoots it. The more I watch, the more excited I am to see her play in a game. Funny that I never thought of hockey before Stone. It just seems so violent. I'm sure I'll be cringing the first game I see, especially if she gets checked. I don't even watch football because there is entirely too much contact. As a physical therapist, I'm focusing more on the possible injuries than the game. I've stopped watching all sports.

"Elizabeth, I have to go to work now." I raise my voice so she can hear me. She heads over to me, her blue eyes shining. It's nice to see her in her element and genuinely happy.

"I'm sorry. There's no Elizabeth here."

"Elizabeth." I take a step back from the railing. "You're doing well on the ice. I'm proud of how far you've come." She skates to a hidden door. I squeal when I realize she is too quick for me and I'm trapped. She slowly takes off her gloves.

"No Elizabeth here." On skates, Stone is very intimidating. And very tall. I know the worst that will happen here is that she'll kiss me senseless.

"I like Elizabeth. It's a pretty name," I say, trying to somehow redeem myself. She towers over me. She's so close that I have no choice but to reach out to her. She captures my hands and puts them around her waist.

"I tell you what. You can call me Elizabeth, but only in private. Deal?" She leans down and kisses me before I have a chance to answer. It's the kind of kiss that makes me clutch her tighter. When we break apart, I'm breathing hard.

"Deal." I say. We both smile. "Don't overdo it." I look around to make sure nobody is around even though I know we are alone. "Elizabeth." She pokes my side and I bust out laughing. "Okay, okay. Only in the privacy of us." She kisses me again.

"Have a good day. I'll call you later." She winks at me and heads back to the ice. This Stone I can get used to. I tell myself to calm down and try to not act like a teenager with a crush.

❖

You want to come to the season opener as my guest?

I love that she only texts me during my lunch. It's so considerate.

I would love to. Thank you.

The season opener against the Boston Pucks happens to be the date I was going to marry Alison. I have mixed feelings about that day. I'm disappointed in myself for not caring more about our breakup. I'm not heartless, I'm just sure that I did the right thing. Jumping into something right away with Stone wasn't smart, but it feels good.

I still don't know a thing about hockey though. What if I'm bored?

She's quick to respond. *You won't be bored, I promise.*

That makes me smile. I know that it will be exciting and I'll catch on, but I'm also going to be a nervous wreck. Hopefully, she and her coach know her limits. I know Stone has a lot to prove out on the ice, but I'm confident she will be smart about it.

If I am, you have to make it up to me. Saturday nights are too valuable to just throw away on watching women chasing after a ball or whatever it's called. There are so many good books to read. I'm falling behind in my book club.

I laugh because she knows I know it's a puck. I smile and wait for her response.

"Look at you all happy and shit." Gloria walks into my office and stares at me. "What's going on?"

I scramble around in my brain and try to come up with something, anything. "One of my friends just was razzing me about something." All truths. Stone is a friend and she was just giving me a hard time. "What's going on?" Deflect, deflect.

"Just checking in with you. You seem well and that makes me happy." She sits in one of my chairs. I offer her coffee because that's our thing, but she declines.

A thought pops in my head that chills me. What if she knows about me and Stone? Not that I think we've done anything wrong, but I know I should tell Gloria. She needs to hear it from me. I owe that to her. Just not today. What if Stone told her parents and her parents told Gloria? I test the waters carefully. "I'm good. I'm tired today, but happy it's almost the weekend. What are your plans?"

"Political Pete has a dinner tonight that I'll attend." I love that even though she makes fun of her husband's political career, she really is proud of him. "I'm envious of you. I just want to go home, take a long bath, read a book, and go to bed early. Oh, how's the house? Have you made peace with it?" she asks.

"It's good. Thanks again for recommending it to me. I needed something quick and it's perfect. By spring, I'll have a better idea of where I want to live. The suburbs are hard if you're single."

She nods. "I agree. Too bad you didn't get the condo. That was a great place."

"I'm sure I'll find something just as great somewhere else. I'm not worried."

"Enjoy your weekend. I'm sneaking out early to get my hair done. I'm leaving you in charge." She tells everybody that when she leaves early. I roll my eyes at her.

"Don't embarrass your husband. Again," I say. She busts out laughing. Last political dinner she attended, she walked around the entire function kissing babies and shaking hands with toilet paper stuck to her heel. I still laugh thinking about it. She waves and disappears.

I pick my phone back up because it buzzed several times while Gloria and I were chatting.

Stone sent me three texts. *If you hate the game, I'll make it up to you. I promise.*

I don't know when I'll be able to see you this coming week. Our practices are early morning and evening.

This is why it's hard to have a relationship. I'm sorry.

I feel bad that I left her hanging for so long because of Gloria's impromptu visit. I quickly respond.

Sorry. Boss was here. We'll find time to see one another. I'm not worried. I throw on a happy face to ease her mind.

I know she will have time off during the season and I've been known to stay up late a time or two. She obviously doesn't remember that I was engaged to a surgeon. I know all about late nights, early mornings, and crazy long hours.

Chapter Twenty-three

I'm feeding off the crowd. It's crazy at the arena. I never knew hockey was this popular. There are so many kids here, it makes me smile. Tonight is the home opener and they are giving away T-shirts to all kids twelve and under. I buy a Gray Wolves' sweatshirt to show my support, then find my seat. I'm a few rows up from the Gray Wolves' bench and can see everything clearly.

The pre-show is hilarious as the wolf mascot chases Boston's mascot around the ice. The team even has cheerleaders. That surprises me. It's a sold out crowd. I have a feeling I have one of the best seats in the house. When the opposing team takes the ice, the crowd boos. So much for good sportsmanship. The Gray Wolves take the ice and the crowd jumps up, screams, and whistles. When Stone is introduced, the smile on my face couldn't be any larger. She is definitely the most popular. The mascot high fives her and hands her crutches. She shakes her head and refuses them. The crowd goes wild. She twirls to show him that she is good to play and he falls to his knees to bow to her. The crowd eats it up. I feel like I'm floating. The most popular girl in the room is mine. Sort of.

Stone doesn't start the game, but subs a few times. I hold my breath when she takes the ice. I can tell she's worried, but she keeps up and manages to get a few shots at the goal. They are evenly matched teams, but I can tell that if Stone was one hundred percent, they would have points up on the board already. The first time she gets checked, I'm scared. The second time, I'm livid. The player on the other team actually pulls her down to the ice and gets a penalty card. Stone hops up and skates away as if it didn't bother her at all. The coach calls her in. She's seems frustrated that she hasn't scored, but keeps her anger in check. Her tense jaw and still form are a dead giveaway. I can't decide if I want the coach to put her back in so she can expel that energy, or keep her out so that she has more time to rest. The few minutes she played was aggressive and I know her leg has to hurt.

Just when I think the game is over, I find out there are two intermissions. We've just reached the first one. No wonder Stone said she would never see me on the weekends. A hockey game takes forever. I get up to stretch and find something to eat. I indulge in a pretzel with cheese and a beer. It's only a matter of time before I hit the cotton candy. I find my seat again before the craziness starts. I'm having a good time. It's hard to be here alone, but the fans around me are very nice and friendly. Stone starts the second period and plays for five minutes. The score is one to one. I know that winning the first game usually sets the tone for the season in all sports. I really hope Stone scores. That will do so much for her ego and self-confidence. This game is moving so fast. It's hard to find the puck and who has it if you don't know where to look for it. I don't understand the rules yet.

"It just takes time to learn everything. Think of it as soccer on ice," the lady in front of me explains. Well, that's no better.

I shrug at her. "I'm just not a sporty person I guess. I'm sure I'll pick it up. This is only my first game. I understand the concept, just not all of the penalties and some of the calls."

"Who do you know on the team?" she asks.

I cringe. I really want to keep a low profile. "A friend of mine had an extra ticket and offered it to me. These are really nice seats. Do you have season tickets?" I'm deflecting.

"Not really season tickets, but I get tickets to all of the games. My daughter plays. She's number five, the back-up goalie. This section is reserved for family of the Gray Wolves."

I can tell she's sizing me up and trying to figure out who gave me their ticket. I ignore her blatant staring and focus on the game. All is forgotten when the Wolves score. I look down at the bench and can tell Stone is itching to go back in. She's benched for the rest of the second period. I get up and walk around during the second intermission. Nobody leaves early. The place is just as packed now as when the game first started.

When the third period starts, the fans get crazy. This is it. The Wolves just need to keep their lead or increase it. Stone is in and I can barely contain my excitement. She fights for the puck and the player who checks her into the wall gets tangled up in her own skates and falls down. It's just her against Boston's goalie. I'm dying right now. The crowd is so loud and Stone is so driven and fast that I don't know if I should focus on her or the puck. She is headed full speed at the goalie and at the last second, veers right and taps the puck into the net behind the goalie. Score! It's perfect.

Her teammates pile around her to celebrate. She skates to the sidelines and, before she sits on the bench, turns and winks. I know it's for me, even though every other woman in this area probably thinks that the wink was for her. I'm so happy. I watch her loosen her skate and I know she's done for the day. I hope she's okay. Mentally, yes, but I'm more concerned with her physical well-being.

The Gray Wolves end up winning four to two. Stone and I didn't really talk about what we were going to do, if anything, after the game so I head to my car and leave. I know that there will be a team meeting, then showers so she won't be available for at least an hour. Once I'm out of the parking lot, it only takes fifteen minutes to get to my house. That's not bad at all. I strip down and shower because I spilled some beer during one of the many times I jumped to celebrate or encourage the team. I'm happy that I have a Gray Wolves' sweatshirt. It makes me feel closer to Stone. I throw on a tank top and some boxers and crawl under the covers. The game was a lot of fun. I'm glad I went. Now that I've seen Stone in her true element, I'm so happy I was involved in helping her heal.

Chapter Twenty-four

"Hello?" My cell phone wakes me up, but when I see it's Stone, I don't complain.

"Were you asleep? I'm so sorry. I'll leave."

"Wait. Where are you?" I sit up in bed, my heart beating furiously. She's here.

"I'm outside. It's okay. I'll talk to you tomorrow," she says, her voice low as if she's trying to not wake me up.

"Don't move. I'll be right there." I jump up and look around for my robe. It's short, mid-thigh, but it covers more than what I wore to bed. I slip that on and run to the bathroom to look at myself. The light is too bright so I flip it back off. I need to calm down. I take a deep breath, tighten the sash, and head for the door.

"Go back to bed. I'm so sorry I woke you up." Stone takes a step back from me. I reach out for her.

"Get in here, superstar."

She laughs when I grab her jacket and pull her inside. I shut the door. When I turn, she is right behind me. She leans down and kisses me. I know her energy is amped from the game earlier. I felt it the second I touched her. Her clothes are cool against me, but her body is warm. Always so warm. Our kiss deepens and I move closer to her. I don't even notice that she has untied the sash of my robe until I feel her warm hands on my waist. I slide my hands up to the back of her head. Her hair is still damp from her shower. She smells heavenly. I moan because I want her.

I slide off her jacket and pull her toward my bedroom, kissing and touching her. Somewhere along the way, I lose my robe. She stops us in the hallway and presses me against the wall. After thoroughly kissing me, she lifts me up. I wrap my legs around her hips and press myself into her. She pushes back into me, grinding her hips hard and fast. I break our kiss to catch my breath. I don't want to come this way. She has other plans though. She moves her hands underneath me so that her fingers are on my pussy. My shorts are drenched. I should feel ashamed at my body's reaction to her, but after hearing her guttural moan at finding me so wet, I feel empowered instead. I wiggle against her hand, wanting to feel her inside of me instead of teasing me through my clothes. She lifts me away from the wall and walks us into my bedroom.

"Stone, your leg. You shouldn't carry me." By the time I get the sentence out, she's already at the foot of the bed. She leans down until I'm on my back and shuts me up by kissing me again. I want to feel her skin and her heat against my body so I slip my hands between us to unbutton her shirt. She slides her hand up my tank top to rest on my stomach. I stop because she stops. "What's wrong?"

"Nothing at all. I just want to look at you." I can't even imagine what I look like to her. It can't be great. My hair is probably a tangled mess, my clothes are half off, and I'm rubbing up against her for relief. I put my hands over my face because I'm utterly embarrassed. She moves my hands away. "What are you doing?"

"I'm a mess and I'm moving entirely too fast for us. I'm sorry," I say.

Stone leans down and kisses me softly. "No, you aren't. Make no mistake. We're going to have sex. I'm going to touch you and kiss you everywhere. I just wanted to see your face since I didn't get to see it much today." She runs her fingertips over my cheeks, down my jaw, across my lips, and back up the other side. I shiver and I don't even hide it. "You're beautiful. Everywhere." She breaks eye contact to look at the rest of me.

I'm trying hard not to shake. My body is tingling. My emotions are raw. I've never been sure of wanting another person this much in my entire life. She runs her fingers gently over my tank, barely brushing my hard nipples. I arch my back into her touch, but she doesn't give me what I want. Her hand moves lower on my stomach, brushing the top of my shorts which are now barely covering me. It's so hard to remain still, but I know this is something Stone wants to do. I can't help moaning though. I lean up and tug her earlobe into my mouth, sucking it hard, biting it softly.

She presses her hand against me and slips underneath my waistband. Her fingers slide over my mound and cup it, her fingertips brushing my wet slit. She turns her head and kisses me. Her tongue is warm and possessive and I submit to her. She slides a finger inside of me and I push my hips down into her hand. I want her deeper inside of me. I spread my legs apart to give her room and she adds a finger. I moan at how full she feels inside of me. She moves slowly and I rock my hips against her hand.

"You are so tight and so wet," she says against my mouth.

I open my eyes and watch her watch me. Her face is serious and her eyes so intense. "You feel so good. So good." I close my eyes again. My body adjusts to her quickly and I start moving my hips faster.

I need her. I need all of her. I finish unbuttoning her shirt and tug at her belt. I'm not going to be able to take off her clothes because I'm too weak. She slips out of me to remove her clothes. Her shoes take her awhile to unlace and she groans in frustration. I sit up on my knees and lean over her shoulder to kiss her neck, her cheek, the soft spot behind her ear. She reaches for my hand and places a gentle kiss on my palm. When she pulls off her boots, she stands to shrug off her shirt and jeans. She reaches out for me wearing a sports bra and boy shorts. Black is definitely her color. She looks dangerous and chiseled.

I reach out and run my fingers over her muscular abs. She quivers under my touch. She's brimming with need and I'm so wet and ready that I'm two seconds away from touching myself. She crawls up, pushing me down on the bed, and places wet kisses on my body. When she settles between my legs, I moan at the contact and spread my legs even further to accommodate her. I reach up and hold her to me, my arms on her strong shoulders. She is solid and beautiful. She sits up and pulls me with her so she can take off my tank top. I'm worried about her ankle and leg at this angle.

"I feel fantastic. Don't worry." She runs her fingers over my frown. "I promise that I couldn't be any better right now." She gently lowers me back onto the bed and pulls down my shorts. I'm completely naked now and I shiver. "Are you cold?"

"No. I just…I just need you." She slides over me, covering my body with hers. Her weight is perfect on me. She leans down and kisses me hard. I love how well we kiss. Most couples take time learning how to kiss one another. Stone and I knew from our first kiss. My lips are swollen and tender and I don't even care. She lifts her body off of mine a few inches and is holding herself up on her elbows and knees. "Please?" I look up at her, missing her heat and her hardness.

She nudges my legs further apart and slides two fingers back inside of me. I gasp and moan loudly. She watches me as she builds me up. I feel completely helpless and in her control. I bring her lips to mine. She kisses my mouth, my jaw, my neck, and moves lower down my body. I try to slow my orgasm down because I want to come with her mouth on me. She runs her tongue across my breasts and kisses a trail down to my thighs. I dig my fingers into her hair and push her gently down. I can feel her smile against my body.

"I told you I couldn't wait to taste you." She gently pulls out of me and pushes my legs up, both hands now at the back of my knees, and leans down to lick me from the bottom of my slit all the way to the top. I whimper with need as her mouth finds my core and her strong tongue thrusts inside of me. She releases my legs, but continues to move her tongue in and out. It's decadent and I want more. She runs her warm hands up my thighs, across my stomach to cup my breasts. I don't even realize I'm touching them until her hands brush mine away. She moves her mouth up to my clit, and her warm, wet tongue circles it and guides it into her mouth. She is devouring me and I'm only seconds away from coming. My hands find her hair and I hold onto her as I climb each wave higher and higher, moaning louder and louder. She slips her fingers back inside of me and slowly pumps in and out. I squirm and beg for more, so close to coming. She increases her speed until I cry out as my orgasm crashes into me. My skin is covered in a thin layer of sweat and I'm shaking. She covers me with her body and places tiny kisses on my cheeks, my hair, and my neck. I hold onto her tightly as I ride each wave out.

"Oh, my God." That's all I can say right now. My brain is still trying to process everything that happened.

"Thank you," she whispers against my cheek.

That's crazy. She's thanking me? She just delivered me a screaming orgasm and she's thanking me? "I should be thanking you. That was incredible."

"Thank you for answering your door, then." She sprinkles my face with tiny kisses, then kisses me slowly, thoroughly. I taste myself on her lips. I feel tears stinging behind my eyes. I can't cry right now. Why am I crying? Stone leans up to look at me. She wipes the tears gently off of my cheek. "Please tell me I didn't hurt you or rush you into this." I cry harder because I'm overwhelmed by feelings I haven't sorted out yet. I shake my head to give her an answer because I can't stop crying long enough to explain. She rolls us over so I'm on top and holds me close. She touches my hair, rubs my back, and pulls the comforter over us. Finally, after five minutes of me having a meltdown, I'm able to talk.

"I'm so sorry I ruined our night. I didn't expect to cry and I don't know how to explain myself," I say.

She kisses me softly. "Are they good emotions?" She gently rolls me over and suddenly sits up. "I'm so sorry. I forgot about what today was. I'm such an asshole."

I look at her like she's crazy. "What are you talking about?"

"You were supposed to get married today." Stone drops that between us. That didn't even cross my mind tonight, not even at the game. Maybe subconsciously, but that's not the reason why I'm crying. How do you tell somebody you just started a relationship with that you are falling for her? It's entirely too soon. Even I know that. If I said anything to Stone, she would bolt. I look at the clock. It's twelve fifty.

"Yesterday. My wedding was supposed to be yesterday. Please. I'm not emotional about that. I honestly forgot. I just…" I don't know what to tell her without sounding clingy. "This was really nice. Sometimes I've a hard time expressing myself and I cry. Please come back."

She looks at me warily. "Are you sure?"

I nod. "I promise, but…" She stops. "You need to be completely naked." That puts a smile on her face. She gets up to take off her sports bra and her boy shorts, and slips back into bed next to me. I can't wait to touch her. She's so hard and soft at the same time. I run my hands all over her body. She is so warm and tense.

Her moans encourage me the closer I get to her thighs. She spreads herself for me as I crawl between her legs. Her hips move as soon as my mouth finds her wet core. I want to please her. I hold her hips down with my hands. She moans and tries hard not to buck against me, but she is already close to coming. I let go of her hips and rub my fingers up and down her wet slit. She pushes against me. I slip one finger inside of her, marveling at her tightness. She hisses out her approval so I continue moving in and out of her, my mouth still firm on her swollen and slick clit. Within seconds she cries out. Her entire body shakes with release.

I place tiny kisses on her thighs and work my way back up until I can kiss her on her lips. She is still breathing hard and holds me close. I rest my head on her shoulder and listen to her speeding heart slow with every heavy breath. I can't stop myself from touching her. I'm fascinated with her body. I know it so well, but I'm really learning it for the first time.

Chapter Twenty-five

I wake up alone. I crack an eye at the clock. It's eight thirty-three. I feel like I need another four hours of rest. What time did we finally go to sleep? I sit up and wonder if Stone is still here. I can't imagine she would leave without telling me. Did she and I slept through it? I drag myself to the bathroom for a quick primping session in case she's still here. I grab fresh shorts and a T-shirt and head for the kitchen. Stone's sitting at the kitchen table, her leg propped up on another chair and wrapped in ice. She's engrossed in something on her phone and doesn't hear me come in.

"You should have woken me up." I walk toward her. "How's your ankle?"

She grabs for me when I walk by her and pulls me into her lap. "Good morning, you. I figured you needed sleep. You are, after all, older than I am." She kisses me soundly.

I poke her side. "Older and wiser. Did you get any sleep at all?" I lean over and kiss the corner of her mouth. I blush, remembering the last nine hours of my life.

"Yes. I don't need a lot of sleep. Plus, we have a game and I have to get to the arena by ten," she says.

I jump up. "I forgot about that. I'm going to cook you breakfast. Please. It's the least I can do." She follows me into the kitchen, her hands still on me. "Elizabeth, go sit down or make coffee."

She pulls me to her. "Thank you. Last night was very special for me." She places a delicate kiss on my lips.

"For me, too. Are you okay with everything?" I don't even know what that means. "I know it was kind of fast and we were going to wait."

"It was perfect. Really. The game, you, us. I wouldn't change anything," she says.

I smile and slip out of her arms. "Sit down, champ. I need to cook you breakfast for your big game today." She relents and heads back to the table. I know she is watching me. I'm positive I will always be aware of her. Her intensity is hard to miss. I find that I like her watching me. I gather up ingredients for scrambled eggs and bacon. She nods her head in approval. I get the bacon hot and sizzling before starting the eggs. "Are you good with toast?"

"Definitely. Can I at least make that?" I nod and she jumps up, anxious to help.

"So tell me about your game today. Who are you playing? How is your ankle? Do you think the coach will put you in?"

"And the last lesbian on Earth who didn't know anything about hockey is now excited about it." Stone raises her arms in victory and makes tiny, quiet celebratory noises.

"What's my prize?" I ask.

Her body presses against mine. Her hands run down the curves of my waist until they reach my hips. She pulls me back into her, the intent obvious. She nuzzles my neck, then moves her lips up to my ear. "Whatever you want," she whispers. I shiver. She tightens her grip on my hips, then releases me only to run her hands down my shorts.

"It's really hard to concentrate on not burning your food when you're touching me like this." I have to put both hands on the stove to keep from falling forward.

"Am I a distraction?" She turns my face toward her to kiss me. I lean back, my lips captured by hers in a demanding and passionate kiss. I break it only to look at the food on the stove, which is starting to look and smell a little done.

"I just want to give you a nice breakfast since you have a busy afternoon. Toast," I command. She backs away, her hands up in the air as if surrendering, and pops the bread into the toaster.

"I'll eat anything you want me to." Her double entendre and wicked smile doesn't deter me from salvaging breakfast. I pour orange juice and milk while she butters the toast.

"This is a lot of food," she says after I fix our plates.

"Yeah, I probably went overboard, but I really don't know what you need before a game."

"Carbs and protein. Some fruit." She stops me when I get up to slice some grapefruits and oranges. "Orange juice is fine. I did eat pasta last night so I still have carbs to burn. This is perfect, Hayley."

I sit back down, still worried that I haven't prepared the right kinds of food. "Bacon probably isn't on your list."

She laughs and stares at the five pieces on her plate. "I love bacon. Don't take it away from me. That's just cruel."

"I'll know better for next time you're here."

"So there'll be a next time?" she asks.

"It's a good thing you have a game because if you didn't, we would not be in the kitchen right now. We'd be back in the bedroom getting to know each other better." I'm rewarded with the genuine smile that makes my heart tremble. Ignoring the throbbing of my libido, I try to keep the conversation mature and not worry if I satisfied her. I'm assuming I did something right because she's still here. Last night is such a blur. "What does the team normally do after Sunday games?"

"We'll hang around for autographs and photos with the kids. I should be done by six," she says.

"Would you like to come over and watch a movie tonight? I mean, if you aren't doing things with the team. Only if you have time or want to." Could I sound a little more desperate right now?

"I'd love to see you again. Let me bring dinner over since you cooked breakfast." She smiles. I love her smile.

"Only if you have time." I look at the clock. She gets up and walks to me. She reaches for my hand. I think she is going to kiss me, but she pulls me up and holds me.

"I can't wait. I will see you at six and I'll call if there's a problem, okay?" She grabs her coat and heads out the door.

The whole time I'm cleaning the kitchen, I have a cheesy, satisfied grin on my face. Last night was perfect. Stone had an amazing game that I got to see, and when she showed up, we both immediately knew what was going to happen. My bedroom still smells like sex. I know I should change the sheets, but I crawl into them again and decide that a quick nap before a shower could only make this day more perfect.

Chapter Twenty-six

I smile when the doorbell rings at five thirty. Stone is early. Thankfully, I'm dressed and ready for her. I open the door and find Alison instead.

"Alison. What are you doing here?" My cheeks heat up and my fists clench.

"I want to talk. Can I come in?"

"Actually, no. I was just on my way out." I just want her to leave. I don't want my past and my present to cross paths.

"Just for five minutes. I promise. I will leave in five minutes," she says.

I relent and let her in. "How did you find me?" I ask. I need to know whose ass to kick.

"It doesn't really matter," she says. I can't imagine Gloria telling her. Maybe Tina did. Alison sits on the couch. "Look, I've done a lot of thinking and I know I can change. I miss you. I miss us. Maybe we can try therapy or even start over. There has to be something I can say or do." She looks miserable. I believe that she misses me, but it doesn't change anything. If I thought we could do something to salvage our relationship, then I would have suggested it.

"I'm sorry, but I just don't think so. I miss you, but not us. This is something I had to do. I feel good about myself again. I hope you understand that. I'm not trying to hurt you, but I have to be honest." At least now I can look at her while we talk. Last time, I couldn't. She still looks sad, but she also looks determined.

"I hate the thought that we're going to walk away from one another. We get along so well. We like to do the same things, we have a lot in common, and we have the same friends." She reaches out to me, but I pull back.

"I don't think we—" The doorbell rings. I want to die. This cannot be happening. I answer the door because as much as I want to run away, I can't.

"Hi. Are you okay? You look really pale," Stone says. I give her a nervous laugh before I step back and allow her to enter. "I'm sorry. I didn't know you had company."

"Stone, this is Alison. Alison, this is Stone." I say.

"Hi. Oh, hey. You play for the Gray Wolves, right?" Alison asks. How does every single person know about hockey except for me?

"Right. Hi. Nice to meet you," Stone says. She quickly turns to me and says in a low voice, "Do you need me to leave?"

"No, please stay. Alison was just leaving." I sound heartless, but she came over unannounced and uninvited. Thankfully, Alison takes the hint and heads for the door.

"Please call me. I'd like to continue this later. Nice to meet you, Stone." She leaves and I can't close the door fast enough.

I turn to Stone. "I'm so sorry about that. I had no idea she was coming over. I have no idea how she found out where I'm living." I'm trying not to be upset, but it's so unsettling. I didn't want her to know where I live for this very reason. She's such a control freak and she came over just to rattle me. That's what she does if she doesn't get her way. She's relentless and irritating as fuck. Stone reaches out and I lean into her for strength and warmth.

"I'm sorry. I'm sure that wasn't easy. Are you okay?" She's so concerned about me and I feel like crying, but I know that if I do, Stone will take it the wrong way. I manage to keep it together and paste a smile on my face.

"Yeah, I was just so excited for tonight and she put a damper on my mood." Stone hugs me. I smile at the familiarity of her scent.

"Let's not let her ruin tonight, okay? It's been such a good day."

"Oh! Did you win your game?" I completely forgot that her second game was today.

"We did. I didn't score, but I also didn't get a lot of playing time. I wanted to rest my leg from last night's game." That concerns me.

"Are you okay? Is your ankle tight?" I turn into a doctor immediately and make her sit on the couch. I order her to take off her shoes while I head to the kitchen for an ice pack. Her leg is propped on the couch when I return. "You know, all you have to do is ask if you want one of my massages."

She smiles at me. "Doc, I can't wait for a massage, but the other kind. You know, the kind where you aren't trying to rip my leg off. The kind where maybe massage oil is involved and other parts of my body are explored." Bad mood gone.

"Maybe we should eat first since the food is still hot."

She responds with a groan, but nods. She kisses me quickly and jumps up to get plates from the kitchen while I investigate the contents of the large brown bag.

"Chicken pot pie from the restaurant next to my building. Very yummy and I promise you will love it. Any thoughts on a movie?"

"What do you like to watch? Romance, thrillers, comedies, science fiction?" I ask.

"Yes."

"No preference? Or are we going to have to watch something like *Rudy* or *We Are Marshall* or *Miracle*?"

She laughs. "Why? Because I'm a dumb jock and I only watch tearjerker sports underdog movies? In all fairness, they're pretty good choices, but I'll watch anything really. It's nice to just decompress in front of mindless television."

We scroll through the new releases on Netflix and settle on a science fiction about aliens versus humans. Stone's eyes light up when we start it. Soon enough, she'll find out that I agreed to the movie because it's an excuse to sit close to her and have her hold me if I get scared. The movie starts and I make her put her ankle in my lap so I can give her a massage.

My emotions are still all over the place. I wish Alison hadn't put a damper on my spirit for tonight because I had something entirely different in mind. Stone's ankle is swollen so I'm careful with it.

"I've missed your touch, Doc." She closes her eyes for a minute.

"Remember when you hated this?"

She cracks her eye open at me. "Oh, this is still painful, but I got used to it, so it's welcome," she says.

I massage her for another twenty minutes, then gently place the ice bag on her ankle. "How's your leg? I've been focusing so much on your ankle." She pulls up her pant leg up to her knee. "I still think the surgeon did a great job on your stitches. You have minimal scarring and this'll be a great conversation piece in the summer when you wear shorts."

"I have zero problems with my leg. You'd think that a break that required surgery would take longer to heal than a fractured ankle."

"All of your weight is on your ankle though. Plus, it twists and turns and we need to make sure it does all of that for the rest of your life."

"I know. I just want to whine a little bit," she says. I try not to smile. Stone is one of the strong ones. When the movie ends, Stone leans forward and kisses me softly. "I'm going to go home, okay?"

I nod. Tonight didn't work out the way I wanted it to. I wanted to pick up from where we left off this morning, but Alison had to show up and ruin the night. "I'm sorry our night fizzled out."

She pulls me to her and holds me. She is warm and comforting so I circle her waist with my arms and lean into her. "It's okay.

Tonight was nice. I like spending time with you and just being us, you know?"

I nod. "Thanks for understanding. Dinner was nice. Thank you for treating." She kisses the end of my nose.

"Get some sleep. I'll talk to you tomorrow sometime." I watch her get into her car and drive away. I frown and close the door. This day started on such a high note and ended with such a resounding thud.

Chapter Twenty-seven

"How was your weekend?" Gloria walks into my office and sits on the couch.

"It was okay. Alison found me and stopped by last night," I say.

Her mouth drops open. I mentally mark Gloria off of the list. Not even Meryl Streep could pull off the look on her face right now. "You're shitting me," she says. I shake my head. "So what happened? I mean, if you feel like talking about it." She sits back in the chair and looks at me like she couldn't care less, but I know she's dying to know.

"There was a knock on my door and she was there. I don't know how she found me and she wouldn't reveal her source. We only talked for a few minutes. You can't just show up unannounced at somebody's house and expect them to be agreeable, especially given our circumstances." I leave the part out about Stone showing up a few minutes later.

"What did she say?"

"She told me she missed me and is willing to try to change to make me happy. I told her no, but I don't think I've heard the last of her." I sit back in my chair and sigh. "I mean, I wouldn't mind being friends with her, but I think we're a long way from that."

"I get where she's coming from. You were her rock. She's missing her foundation. On the flip side, I haven't seen you this content in a long time. You do look tired today, though," she says.

"It's too bad my boss is here or else I'd curl up on my couch and take a little nap."

"Your boss sounds like such a bitch," she says.

I nod and am rewarded with a wadded up piece of paper that almost lands in my coffee. "She has her moments. Most of the time, she's pretty okay though."

❖

What are you doing Thursday? I want to take you on a hayride at the orchard.

Stone's texts always make me smile.

That sounds like fun. I'm in.

Great. I'll pick you up at six.

I'm sure we'll talk before then. I'm still upset about our night getting ruined. The sex was really good and I'm anxious to go back to that closeness with her. Stone makes me feel things I haven't felt in a long time; treasured, important, desired. I've missed feeling wanted. I know Alison loved me, but I can't remember feeling this excited about spending time with another person. Passion. It's real and it's been missing in my life.

I keep the conversation going because I miss her. *So we aren't going to talk until then?* My phone rings almost immediately. I answer it. "You didn't have to call me. I was just playing." The background sounds loud so I know she's at a rink.

"How are you?" Her voice soothes me.

"A little tired because I stayed up too late reading, but good. Are you skating today?"

"I had PT this morning, so I'm getting ready to hit the ice. My ankle feels good and my leg feels good. This might be the week everything clicks into place for me." During one of our first sessions, I told her that some athletes know the exact moment when they are one hundred percent. I've heard this more than once. I think just hearing that really helped Stone push herself to heal.

"That's fantastic. Maybe your coach will let you start?" I'm hopeful. She did have a good game on Saturday and thought she did well yesterday, too.

"I hope so. Our practices will be tough, but I'll show her that I can get back out there. I know all of our plays already. I just need to be able to execute them. We have two new players and I don't know how we mesh yet."

"The kindergartners?" I laugh at her growl.

"They're young and really fast. I'm going to have to push myself hard just to keep up with them. Thank God I'm the tallest on the team. That gives me a bigger reach." I shiver recalling how tall and how strong Stone is. She picked me up in my hallway and carried me to the bed in only a few steps. I need another night like that. Several, in fact. "Will I get to see you before Thursday?" she asks.

"Yes." That sounds desperate. "I mean, I don't have anything planned this week except Thursday. I have a date with a hot chick in some hay."

She laughs. "Lucky you. How are you doing after everything that's happened?" For a moment, I think she is talking about the incredible sex we had and just as I'm about to embarrassingly moan out an answer, my brain reminds me that Alison stopped by last night and she probably is referring to her untimely visit.

"I'm okay. I'm sorry that Alison showed up and ruined what would have been the perfect weekend." Stone doesn't deserve this. She deserves somebody who doesn't have baggage like I do. We really should have waited, but we are already in it. "I'm still cringing about it. I'm sorry you had to see that," I say.

"It's okay. I know your history. I'm just sorry it made you sad last night," she says.

And I thought I was masking my emotions well. "I wasn't sad. I was upset that she ruined my night. Our night."

"Saturday was a great night, in case I didn't say anything before." Her voice is low and smooth and I cover my face with my hand as I remember that warm voice whispering things in my ear that nobody has ever said to me before. It was erotic and with anybody else, would have made me blush. Stone empowered me. She made me feel sexy and treasured.

"I loved everything about it. I'm just sorry you didn't get enough sleep before your game. Match. What's it called?"

Stone laughs. "What am I going to do with you? If we're going to date, you really need to know the sport. We need to have Hockey 101 classes."

"I promise to be an excellent student. I mean, since you were such a good patient."

"The punishment for not paying attention in my class is severe. Are you sure you want to sign up for that?" Even trying to sound like a disciplinarian, her voice is sexy.

"Definitely. Put me in the front row, teach." I like the playful, less brooding side of Stone.

"Do you want to get together tomorrow night for a little bit? Maybe grab a drink or just hang out? I'd like to show you my place." She sounds shy and adorable.

"Are you trying to pick me up?"

"Is it working? Because if it is, then yes, yes I am," she says.

I've smiled more in the last forty-eight hours than I have all year, I think. "Then I'm in. Tell me your address and I'll meet you after work tomorrow if that's okay." I write down her address and before I know it, my lunch is over and my next patient is here. "I need to go. I'll see you later. Have a great practice." I mentally tell myself to learn as much as I can about hockey and the lingo before tomorrow night.

Chapter Twenty-eight

I cheat and swing by my house to change and clean up after work. My house is on the way to Stone's and I think a quick shower and fresh clothes will pep me up. I'm right. By the time I get to Stone's, I'm only a few minutes late. She lives on the twenty-sixth floor. I'm super excited to see her view.

"I finally made it," I say into the intercom after she answers.

"Who is this? And did you bring treats?"

"Just myself. That should be enough of a treat." I can't believe I just said that. She buzzes me in, and leaves her finger on the buzzer for an extended time to let me know she approves of my answer. Smile.

"Come in," she says when she opens the door. She doesn't move out of my way so my only path is into her arms. I don't hesitate. She feels warm and perfect. "I've missed you."

I look up at her. "I've missed you, too."

She kisses me softly. It's not a passionate kiss, but one that lets me know she's telling the truth. "Let me show you around." She slides her hand down my arms until she is holding my hand and we walk around her place.

It's modest in size and surprisingly down to earth. I was expecting lots of cold, stainless steel, and black. Instead, Stone has hardwood floors and warm earth tones. Her sectional couch is dark sage with colorful pillows. I take an instant liking to it. The master bedroom is gorgeous and I can't wait to sprawl out on her bed. My cheeks heat up just thinking about all of the things I want her to do to me in this room.

"I love your place. It's very comforting and welcoming," I say.

She beams at me. "Thank you. It's not much, but it's not a bad first home." She pulls back the curtains to show me the view of downtown. "Come out here. This is my favorite part."

"I love that you have a balcony." I squeeze past her to step out into the cool night. The city looks so beautiful lit up. "I would be out here every night. Hey, I can see the arena from here." She walks up behind me, places her hands on my shoulders, and pulls me back into her.

"I eat a lot of my meals out here and read when it's light out."

"It's a nice space." I look around. There is a table, two chairs, and a tiny grill. "Perfect really."

"Want to take a walk in the neighborhood? See how single people should live?" I jab her in her side until she laughs.

"The suburbs aren't all bad," I say. She looks at me pointedly. "I was in a bad position. It was the only thing I could find on a day's notice."

"I'm just teasing you. I know. It's a cute house. You've done a nice job with it. Are you going to extend your lease or have you even thought about it yet?"

"No clue really. I need just to take a deep breath because everything is happening so fast," I say.

"I know what you mean. Come on. Let's head downstairs. If you're hungry, we can pick up some sandwiches and some of the best ice cream on Earth." In the hallway, Stone grabs my hand after she locks the door. The businesses downstairs include a dry cleaner, a convenience store, a sandwich shop, and a bicycle repair place.

"Your building is self-sufficient. In case of a zombie apocalypse, I know where to go." She chuckles.

"All the buildings down here have businesses in them. Thankfully, I'm high enough where I don't have to hear them. Sometimes when I'm on the balcony, I hear arguments or celebrations. It's fun being anonymous."

"We definitely hear different things. I hear children playing. And dogs barking. And leaf blowers at the crack of dawn." I'm almost positive now that I will move downtown after the six month lease is up. It puts me closer to Alison, but also closer to Stone. My decision will have to be made with my head and not my heart. I have time though. Plus, everything is still so new with Stone. There's still time to back out before either of us becomes heartbroken. "Show me your neighborhood." A tiny park sits to the side of the condominiums with a walking trail and several fountains. "This is really nice. How long have you lived here?"

"Almost three years since joining the Gray Wolves. I really like it. I thought about getting a bigger place, but I think it's the perfect size for just me." After walking around for almost an hour and seeing Bushnell Arena up close and personal, we stop in an Irish pub for a quick beer and an appetizer.

"How does your leg feel?" She stands up, hops from one foot to the other, showing me how good she feels. Her smile is beautiful. My heart skips a few beats.

"I feel great. Truly. All week long I've been on the treadmill and doing leg lifts. My muscles might not be as strong as they used to be, but I'm catching up fast." I nod. She looks great.

"I want to come to another game. Maybe this weekend?" I ask. She shakes her head.

"I mean yes, but we'll be down in Boston this weekend. Home games are more fun anyway. Road games are hard. We keep our heads down and do our job. That's about all we can do. There are some die-hard fans in the crowd though. I just wouldn't get the chance to hang out with you. The coach keeps us pretty closely under her wing on the road. We have curfews and no men or women in our room policy."

"Shut up. I thought that was fake. You know, only on television."

"Nope. A rule. The coach wants you amped and ready to play. Not satisfied and slow because you just had sex. Plus, there's the whole getting a good night's sleep rule. It shows when you don't."

"I would hate to have anybody dictate when I can have sex or see my girlfriend or wife. It just doesn't seem fair."

"That's why the home games are so much fun. We see our girlfriends or wives and bring them to the games so they can cheer for us and then have sex with us when we go home," she says. I almost believe her until she winks at me before emptying her beer.

"Oh, you." I laugh with her.

"Come on. Let's get sandwiches and relax for a bit. I know you have an early day tomorrow." We head back to her building and grab hot chicken parmesan sandwiches on the way up to her floor. We stand close together in the elevator and I feel like a couple. She is holding my hand and leaning into me. She bends down and kisses me softly. "Thank you for coming over tonight." I reach up and touch her face gently. Her skin is soft and smooth except for the strong line on her forehead. I notice a thin scar and smile. I'm almost positive it's a hockey injury. According to her medical records, all broken bones were from playing hockey. My thumb brushes across her full bottom lip. I lean up to kiss her, but we're interrupted when the ding of the elevator signals we have arrived at her floor. "We can pick this back up in my place."

This I don't doubt. As a matter of fact, I'm hoping it does. It's almost eight o'clock. We seem to be rushed all of the time. I'd like to have a full day with her, preferably in bed, but I'm happy with just dinner and resting my head on her shoulder. Dating. It's everything I remember, only better.

"Tell me about the orchard and this hayride you're taking me on," I say. We sit down on the couch to eat our sandwiches. "Wait a minute, do you have horses on the orchard?" If they do, I didn't see them during the tour.

"No, we'll use the tractor. It's actually really cute. My parents love doing it. It's good business for the orchard."

"I love your parents' orchard. It's great. When you drove me around, I was really impressed with how well it operates and just how adorable it is."

She reaches out to play with my fingers. "Actually, my parents, my brother, and I have equal shares of the business. I figure if the hockey thing doesn't work out for me, I can peddle apples for a living. It's quite lucrative. Ciders, butters, vinegars, snacks. Just so many options."

"I can always bake pies for the business," I playfully suggest.

"No."

"No? Why not?" I ask.

She moves closer to me. "Just no. Nobody gets your pie except for me." She leans to kiss me. I push her back.

"You did not just say that to me."

She laughs and jumps on top of me. "What? That wasn't sexy? I thought for sure you would like that."

"Just call me a broad, too. That'll get my heart thumping fast in my chest," I say.

She's on her hands and knees over me. I scoot down so I'm directly underneath her. "That's hot, right? I thought so."

I pull her down to me so that her lips are right above mine. "So hot." She kisses me. What starts out as playful, turns passionate immediately. I need to feel her against me again so I run my hands up her back and moan when she slides her knees and sinks against my center. "I've missed you."

"I haven't stopped thinking about you and our night since I woke up Sunday." She places tiny kisses on my neck, my cheeks, and the corner of my mouth.

"I'm so sorry our night got ruined."

She silences me with another kiss. "It's okay. We'll have plenty more nights like that. I promise you." Her voice is low and almost a whisper. I believe her. "Maybe right now." We kiss harder. I want this. I want her, I want us. I want to feel the same way I did a few nights ago, wanted and safe.

"Yes." That's the last thing I say for several minutes as she undresses me. I'm dying from her going so slow, but I'm patient because I know I'll be rewarded. I don't even care that I'm down to my panties and bra and she's fully clothed. Between kissing and touching, I'm so ready to come.

"You're so soft and lovely. I've thought about touching you again and again," she says. Her mouth leaves mine to kiss and suck all over my body. She pushes my bra up, not bothering to unclasp it. It's rough and gentle at the same time. I moan and squirm against her, waiting for her mouth to work its way to my nipple. Her teeth scrape my breast, heightening my need. I pull her head into me, begging her to suck hard. She doesn't disappoint. I moan at the pain that's so pleasurable, it makes me squirm harder. She silences me by sliding her hands down my panties and slipping inside me. I push into her hand. I need more already. I want more.

"More." My vocabulary disappears every time Stone touches me. My brain stops functioning. I only need her touch. She slips another finger inside and my hips jerk. Her fingers move deep and I gyrate my hips against her hand. "Oh, God, Stone." I moan over and over. She moves her mouth down my body, gently biting as she goes. She doesn't even make it to my pelvic bone before I cry out as my first orgasm overtakes me.

"I love that you can come this way," she says.

My body's still rocking with the aftershocks. When her mouth finds my core, I spread shamelessly for her. I'm not even close to being done. I'm so wanton with her and I don't care. Her mouth is warm and wet and I move against her, finding the perfect rhythm. I miss her warmth when she slips out of me, but love how strong she grips my legs to hold me in place. I push into her harder and she holds me down, her fingers digging into my thighs. I hear moaning and realize it's coming from both of us. That makes me even more turned on. My second, stronger orgasm rolls over me until I shake.

"I can't believe how incredible you are." She crawls up me again, placing tiny, wet kisses until she reaches my mouth. "You're so beautiful." Her lips are soft against mine, but demanding, and I yield. I hold her close to me.

"You make me feel so special," I manage to say.

"That's because you are."

I smile against her cheek. "All of your clothes are still on. We should change that." She leans up and pulls off her sweater. I reach out to touch her stomach, always amazed at her muscle tone. I help her unbutton her jeans. She stills my hands.

"Let's go back to the bedroom." She pulls me flush against her and kisses me all the way down the hall. I'm surprised she doesn't carry me, but I'm too excited because in about ten seconds, we are going to be rolling around in that giant bed of hers. I look at the clock when we enter her room and am shocked that what happened on the couch took less than fifteen minutes. "Why are you looking at the clock?" she whispers.

"It's still so early. I lose all sense of time with you."

She kicks off her jeans and slips out of her boxers. She didn't even bother with a bra today. Stone just gave me fantastic orgasms, but I want more. I can tell she is nowhere near done with me and I gladly fall on the bed with a playful push from her. She is on me in an instant. I welcome her weight between my thighs. She slips a hand between us and resumes fucking me with her beautifully long fingers. I know that I'm being selfish, but I need her. I need this closeness. I move my hips into her, wanting more friction, bucking against her hard body.

She pushes away from me and as I'm about to ask her what's wrong, she flips me so I'm on my stomach. She runs her tongue along the back of my thigh and I lift up when her mouth hits the curve of my ass. She spreads me and licks my wetness, her hands gripping the back of my thighs. This position is so decadent that I can barely breathe. She grabs my hips and directs me up so that I'm on my hands and knees. Her fingers massage my pussy and I push back into her, wanting, no, needing more. She kneels behind me and drills into me, hard, fast. I cry out as I come again. My legs shake so bad that I can't hold myself up. I collapse onto my stomach. Stone holds my quivering legs.

"Stretch your legs out." She pulls the comforter up over me and pulls me into her arms. She nuzzles my neck and strokes my arms until my breathing slows. I turn so that I'm facing her.

"I don't even know what to say," I say. She runs her fingertips across my cheeks and down my nose. She kisses my lips softly. "You're incredible. Just as fierce and intense in the bedroom as you are out on the ice."

"When I know what I want, I go for it. I want you. Simple as that," she says.

I feel myself melting from the inside out. "Simple, huh? Did you always know you were going to get me?"

"If nothing else, I'm definitely persistent."

"Without a doubt," I say.

She plays with my hair as I stay curled up in her embrace. I'm going to give my body a few minutes to recuperate, plus I like it when she holds me. "I knew I wanted you the moment I saw you." The honesty in her voice is very touching.

"You hated me the moment you saw me."

"I hated life the moment I saw you. I was sure my career was over. My foot wouldn't bend. My leg hurt. I was a complete wreck over that," she says.

I kiss her cheek softly. "You were brave. The best thing to do is know your limits and work your way up from there. I'm thankful you weren't as destructive as you could have been. We've worked with so many athletes who don't follow the plan and end up hurt. It's sad."

"I trusted you. Your kind eyes and gentle demeanor. I knew you were going to help me."

"It's because I gave it to you straight, huh?"

She leans back from me. "What do you mean?"

"I told you I was assigned to work with you since I'm so good with children and most athletes fall under that category."

She laughs and playfully kisses my face. "Truth, Doc. Actually, watching you with your other patients was the best thing that could have happened to me. The kids all were happy even though they had such bad things happen to them. Especially Davis with his prosthetic leg. I can't even imagine."

I don't tell her that I planned for her to be there during his PT. "It's not easy, but I like being a part of the healing process. I know that most of the patients are going to be better after working with us. Especially the kids. They're so much fun and so eager to heal."

"It's because they don't know how to cuss yet," Stone says.

"Oh, trust me. They do know. They just don't know how to give up when they are young."

"Well, thank you for helping me as much as you have. Gloria, too. Don't tell her I said this, but she's tough. It's a good thing I didn't start off with her because I would have bolted after the first week. You are more patient and your voice isn't as loud as hers. She scares me." I smile at her. She lifts my chin so she can kiss me.

I feel adrenaline swell. I gently push her back so I'm on top of her. She holds my hair back from my face so I can kiss her better, harder. I lean down and kiss her neck, her collarbone, and the softness between. Her moans encourage me to continue and I make a path of gentle kisses and light touches all the way to the apex of her thighs. She spreads her legs for me, her hands still wound in my hair, holding me close. Stone isn't shy to share what she likes in the bedroom. I think I'm a fast learner. Judging by her moans and touches, I am.

"Come here," she says. I look up at her, confused that she has stopped me. "Turn around. I want to taste you at the same time." She motions for me to flip around and I don't hesitate.

I'm still tender from my previous orgasms, but the second she brings my core to her mouth, my body tenses and starts racing toward another one. I bury my tongue inside of her and drink her up. Her clit is engorged and hard. She pumps her hips. I hold her down, move my mouth to her clit, and gently suck. Her arms wrap around my waist as she holds me tightly against her mouth. I moan when I hear Stone's noises. Her moans are more like appreciative growls of approval. I run my finger around her opening and gently slip inside of her. She is unbelievably wet and tight. Her walls clench my finger and throb. I know she is close.

I build my orgasm up while licking and sucking her. She bucks into me and her moans get louder and louder. I press harder and start moving my hips against her. Her teeth scrape my clit and I can't stop my own orgasm. I try to stay focused on Stone while my body explodes. Within five seconds of my coming, Stone cries out, too. Her rapid heartbeat pulses against my mouth and my finger. It is beautiful to watch and feel her climax. I place tiny kisses on the inside of her thighs and then turn back around. She pulls me into her arms and kisses my forehead.

"That was fantastic." She sounds breathless and content.

I smile because I'm thrilled. "You are fantastic." I kiss her and twist so I can face her. "My body is drained, yet I feel so alive."

"And it's still early," she says. I lean up over her to look at the clock. It's only nine forty-five. "Plenty of time."

I smile at her. She locks her fingers with mine and pulls me down for a kiss. "Your appetite is remarkable."

"For you? Definitely."

Chapter Twenty-nine

I'm nervous to meet Stone's parents. I know they're going to be there. It is their orchard. They have to know who I am. At some point, I need to pony up and tell Gloria about my budding relationship with our former patient. I'm being a total chicken about it.

"Hi. Are you ready?" Stone wanted to pick me up even though I told her I could meet her at the orchard. She stands in my doorway and pulls me to her for a promising kiss. It leaves me breathless.

I'm still reeling over Tuesday night. It's been my favorite night so far. If we're just getting started as a couple, I'm excited to see where this relationship goes. We haven't discussed being exclusive, but I feel like we don't need to. I know I'm committed and it seems like Stone is as well.

"I am. It's so nice to see you again." I put my arms around her neck and she kisses me again. I love the way she smells and how warm she is.

"You're dangerous, Doc," she says, pushing me back into the house. I know that if we stay here, we might make it back into the bedroom for sex instead of right here in the doorway, but I also know how excited Stone is for the hayride so I stop her.

"You need to stop touching me and kissing me or we'll never leave this place and I do want to go on a hayride with you. This will keep." I moving my finger back and forth between us. She grabs my fingers and brings them to her full lips.

"I'll hold you to that." Her eyes darken and narrow with passion and I shiver knowing what that look means for me. "Come on. Your place is entirely too enticing." She grabs my hand and walks me to her SUV. I love that she opens the door for me every time we're together. I notice a thick wool blanket in the back seat.

"Is that for us, or just something you always have just in case?" A twinge of jealousy pinches my heart.

"It's definitely for us. It's not the softest, but it's the best for a roll in the hay." She wags her eyebrows at me. I shake my head, but laugh nonetheless, relieved that it's for tonight and not for some fan looking for a good time with her. There are certain things I wish I never knew about Stone.

We arrive at the orchard and Stone drives us to one of the barns. The wagons are lined up, ready for this weekend and every weekend until Thanksgiving or the first big snow. It's romantic and beautiful. Stone said that a few years ago, the family even helped plan a wedding proposal.

"I'm going to start up the tractor and bring it around. Hang tight, okay? I'll be right back." She winks and disappears into another part of the barn. I look around. It's very clean and well lit. Obviously, the Stones take great pride in their place and their business. I hear the roar of a diesel engine and see Stone rounding the corner on a beautiful red tractor. It doesn't look like it's been used out in the orchard ever. She backs it up and hitches the wagon to it like a pro.

"How are we going to enjoy the hay if you have to drive us around? I don't want to sit back here by myself. That's no fun. Well, it could be, but I would definitely have more fun with you." That perks her interest.

"Oh, I will make sure we have some alone time. Have a seat and let's get out of here." I adjust the hay into a tiny pile and after spreading out the blanket, I get comfortable. I frown at her when she turns to ensure I'm safely sitting. "It will be totally worth it." I nod, but keep my fake frown on my face. She jumps down to plug something into the tractor and I smile when the wagon lights up.

There are strands of tiny white bulbs along the outside of the frame giving it a warm glow. It's beautiful.

"Oh, Stone. This is perfect. It's so pretty and romantic."

"Come on. Let's go somewhere secluded." She climbs back up into the seat and we head out. It's the perfect night. It's dark, cool, but not chilly, and I can see the stars. I put my hands behind my head and stare up at the night. Stone drives us deeper and deeper into the orchard. I sit up to see how far we are away from the farm.

"You know, if you're going to kill me, you could've fed me first," I say. She tosses me an apple. I laugh. "Something more substantial than one apple." She throws me another one.

"That's the Red Delicious. The one you like snacking on. It should tide you over. Plus, I have a protein bar in my jacket if you're that hungry." It's hard to hear her over the sound of the engine, so I stand up in the wagon and lean forward so that I can talk to her.

"I'm hungry, but not for food." I place a tiny kiss on her neck. I can feel her growl at me, the vibration tickling my lips. I scrape my teeth on her skin.

"In about two minutes, I'm going to pull over and have my way with you." She leans her head back so we can kiss and I feel my body instantly heat up. I'm trying not to make our relationship about sex, but it's so much fun learning her body and opening myself up to her. It's hard not to be turned on knowing what we're capable of. Fantastic things. I wonder if sex is even on the table tonight. Maybe Stone is just doing something nice and romantic.

"One hundred and nineteen, one hundred and eighteen, one hundred and seventeen…" My countdown makes her laugh. She pulls over and I shudder when she shuts off the engine. She climbs over the back of the tractor to hop into the wagon. Her long legs make it look easy. I would have fallen over and busted my head open. "Hi," I say right before she kisses me.

"Hi, yourself. Are you comfortable or should we rearrange things?" I shrug. She's the expert here. She moves some straw around and lies next to me, slipping her arm under my head. We're quiet for a few minutes. "What do you think?" She leans up on an elbow so that she can look down at me.

"This is beautiful. Thank you for tonight." I reach up and touch her chest, right below her collarbone. She leans down and kisses me softly.

"It's the perfect time of year for a hayride. It's cool out so you'll have to snuggle with me to stay warm, but it's not so cold to where you need anything more than a jacket. Plus, we have warm cider in that thermos over there." She points beside me. I didn't even notice it nestled in the hay a few feet away. My eyes light up. Their cider is yummy. Stone laughs and sits up. "I guess you want a sip now?"

"It'll warm me up since your skills are lacking."

She narrows her eyes at me, but still pours me a cup. I sit up to take it from her.

"Those are fighting words. Just so you know," she says. She hands me a glass, but not before licking a tiny drop off of the lip of the cup. I can't help but watch her.

"Your tongue," I say, shaking my head.

"What about it?" The innocence in her voice is enough to make me roll my eyes at her.

"Everything about you is delicious. Especially your tongue." I will always be completely honest with Stone. It's the best way to be after coming out of a relationship that didn't involve a lot of sharing of feelings, thoughts, and dreams.

"You like my tongue, huh?"

I nod. "Very much. I like your full lips and how soft they are, how you kiss, how your mouth can be so gentle and hard at the same time. And the things you do with your tongue." I'm rewarded with a Stone smile. It makes me weak.

"I loved our last date. Not just because we had sex, really good sex, but it's nice to be close to you and touch you the way I want to. Thank you for making this special for me."

"I like how we're happening," I say.

"I know you think we rushed into this, but I hope you feel differently now."

"I should feel guilty about jumping in, but I really don't. My relationship with Alison was over a long time ago, I just didn't know how to end it." I take a deep breath. "Just so you know, I'll have to tell Gloria at some point. I mean, she knows your parents and I'm sure they either know about us or will soon enough."

"I could tell her with you," she says.

"No, I can do it. It should come from me anyway."

"I don't mind going with you. We can tell her together. You're important to me." She smiles sheepishly at that last sentence, her voice dropping low, but I still hear her.

"You're important to me, too, Stone. Okay? I'm having a great time with you. I knew I would. Our chemistry is off the chart." I realize that sounds like it's all about sex so I quickly adjust my words. "I mean, we have a lot in common and we're looking for the same things."

"Hurry up and finish your cider. I want to kiss you again."

I tip my cup back and finish it in five seconds. I'm not about to miss the opportunity to be thoroughly kissed by this woman. I playfully toss the cup over my shoulder and pull her to me. She kisses me softly at first, but deepens it within seconds. We both moan at the same time. Kissing Stone makes me forget about everything. Time, conversation, reality. Right now it's just the two of us underneath these stars and tiny white lights. She takes her time with me. We both know what's going to happen. She slips her hand under my sweater to lightly touch my stomach. I moan my approval. Chills race across my body in anticipation and I arch into her, urging her to continue. I rake my nails lightly at the nape of her neck, something I've learned she likes. My hips automatically push into hers, slowly at first, until we find a steady, deep rhythm. I almost whimper when I feel her hand slide lower and slip between our bodies. She brazenly rubs my mound through my pants and I greedily lift my hips into her touch. Her breath hitches. She quickly unzips my pants and slides her hand between my legs.

"You're so wet already."

I already know this. I'm swollen and slick and I need her inside of me. I'm considering pushing my pants down to my knees, but I like how she is controlling the pace. She leans up on her elbow and watches me. Her eyes widen when she slips inside of me. I can't help but moan and tighten around her. I know she can't get the angle we both want so I push my pants all the way off to give her full access to me.

"Deeper," I say. She leans up over me and pushes two fingers inside of me as deep as she can go. It takes my breath away.

"Is this okay?" she whispers.

I nod, my mouth open, but I can't speak right now. The feeling is so intense and incredible. I pull her to me so I can kiss and moan my approval against her mouth. She speeds up and my hips buck against her. I try to keep them from moving, but I can't. She climbs between my legs and leans over me, her fingers still pumping in and out. Her thighs are keeping mine from jerking around and she is able to go deeper and faster.

I don't want to come yet. I want to stare at her intense face, her blue eyes blazing with determination, and feel her weight on top of me. I want to remember the stars above her, the lights around us, and my heart pounding in my chest. I feel the first quivers and I squelch them, praying my orgasm will hold off. I wrap my hands behind her neck and pull her down to kiss me. I scratch her neck, her back, her waist, trying to get her closer to me. When I finally do succumb, I cry out and ride it for as long as I can. Each orgasm is more intense than the one before. I can't imagine feeling any better than I did Tuesday, but tonight topped it.

"Every time feels different. Better. Does that make sense?" I finally find my voice after several seconds. Stone rests her forehead against mine. Her breath is ragged and her body is brimming with the need to release. I reach down and slip inside of her jeans. She helps me by unbuttoning them. She wants this as much as I do.

"I need to taste you again," I say. She slides off me and leans against a pile of hay beside her. She wastes no time in taking off her boots and jeans. I know she has to be cold so I pull the blanket over her legs, over me, and crawl between her legs. She pushes the blanket off of my head to watch me. That's sexy as hell. I want to please her as much as she has pleased me. Between the angle she's sitting at and the fact that she's so tight, I can really only use my mouth. I hold her open and bury myself in her wetness. She holds my hair and moans as she watches me. It's only a matter of minutes before her hips rock against my mouth and she climaxes.

"I really just wanted to hold you under the stars, but you are too damn sexy and tempting." She's still breathing heavy.

I lean up, scoot closer, and kiss her. "Likewise."

She pulls me gently into her arms. It's tender and romantic, but awkward at this angle. Seemingly sensing my discomfort, she lets me go and hands me my jeans as she reaches for her clothes.

"Just in case somebody shows up," Stone says.

"Well, they're in for a treat if they do." I'm embarrassed, but empowered at the same time.

Stone readjusts the hay and the blanket and turns off the tiny lights. We're submerged in darkness with the twinkling stars above us. It's romantic and somewhat chilly. She pulls the sides of the blanket over us so we're covered. "How well do you know your constellations?" she asks.

"I only know a few. My head was always buried in books and Astronomy wasn't my favorite science."

"I don't know a lot of them either, but different worlds fascinate me, you know?" She points out a few of the popular star clusters. We spend another hour discussing possible life elsewhere and I snuggle deeper against her. I'll always love the smell of Stone. Warm and spicy. "I should probably take you back. It's getting late." I sigh and nod against her. This is nice. I miss her warmth the second she gets up. "Want to sit with me up on the tractor?"

"Is there room for both of us?"

"Sure. Grab the blanket. We just have to make sure it doesn't get caught in the tractor wheels." I shake the blanket of most of the hay and climb on Stone's lap. She doubles the blanket over so it doesn't hang over us and turns on the tractor. I playfully grab her face and hold it against mine.

"Thank you for tonight. It's nice to have a romantic night with you under the stars." I place a tender kiss on her lips to let her know how I feel.

"No, thank you for coming." She smirks. I shake my head at her.

"Brat." She kisses me again.

Chapter Thirty

I want Stone to know that she's on my mind so I text her before her game starts. *Good luck tonight. I'll be thinking of you.*

Thanks. I'm excited to get out there and show them who's boss.

I smile. Stone's energy before a game is off the chart. I know it's just as powerful after a game, too. I'll spend my Friday night with fast food and bad movies. Maybe even a marathon binge of *Buffy the Vampire Slayer*. With the weather changing, I want to hibernate until spring. Stone was lucky she got me out last night. Thankfully, it wasn't too cold. Today, the temperature dropped and I had to dig out my winter coat.

"Hey, you got a minute?" Gloria stands in my doorway looking concerned about something. Shit. She found out about me and Stone.

"Sure. What's up?" My palms are sweating.

"So, you know the Holiday fund-raiser isn't too far away, right?" I breathe out. This isn't about Stone. "Well, I know you want to get more involved in the process since you have more time to yourself, but I just wanted you to know that our point of contact is Alison." The cringe is frozen on her face as she waits for my reaction. Shit.

"Can I do more behind the scenes work? I mean, I can be your backup and have minimal contact with her," I say.

She smiles at me. "Whatever you're comfortable with. You'll have some contact though so know that going in."

Right now, I feel confident and I'm in a budding relationship, so I know I won't have a problem with Alison. "It's okay. I think it will be harder for her than me."

Gloria nods. "Okay, well we will meet next Thursday so if you want to attend, it will be over lunch since we all have busy schedules. I'll just order us food. I know, I know, salads for everyone." She rolls her eyes, knowing how health conscious Alison is.

"I'll have pizza waiting in the wings." In reality, I've lost weight since I moved out. I'm sure it has to do with the stress of everything, but now I eat what I want, within reason, and I don't feel bad physically or mentally.

"Sounds like a plan. Finish your heart attack waiting to happen." She eyes my turkey club croissant sandwich and kettle fried chips.

"Hey, there's fruit here, too." I point to grapes in a baggie.

"Noon. Next Thursday."

Ugh. Our breakup is still relatively new, but hopefully Alison is moving on. I hate that she's our contact. She always told me she was so busy at the hospital. Maybe she wanted to work with us again. Maybe because she knew she would work with me. I don't know, but I'll know the minute I see her face. She's horrible at lying.

My phone buzzes with a text from Rachel. *Hey. What's going on next weekend? I'm headed your way and thought it might be fun to hang out on Saturday.*

Rachel's latest customer is downtown, only about ten minutes from my house. We've already talked about hanging out when she schedules a meet and greet trip.

I'm hanging out with my friend Rachel. Why? I'm so happy she's finally visiting.

Yes! I will be there Thursday and Friday, but not available until late Friday. Will that mess up your plans?

I love my new social life. *No, it's perfect. I'll think of fun things to do.*

I just want to hang out and drink wine. She ends it with a smiley face.

I love her honesty. And her plan sounds perfect. I text her my address. At least now I know to add cleaning my whole place and getting the guest room ready to my list of weekend plans. Sarah Michelle Gellar might have to wait.

❖

It's late but I text Stone anyway.
How was the game?

She doesn't respond. I know hockey nights run late. Plus, I don't know if she had plans with the team after. Hopefully no plans with a fan. I can't imagine that, especially after the last several weeks. Our relationship is moving nicely.

I finish washing the sheets in the guest room and remake the bed. It'll be nice to have a visitor stay here for a night or two. My parents haven't even visited yet. I check my phone a few times hoping Stone texted back, but the only activity is local news advising me of bad weather moving into the area. I decide to get some sleep since it's almost midnight. I'll have to talk to Stone tomorrow.

After seven hours of restless sleep, I drag myself out of bed and head to the kitchen for much needed coffee. I check my phone and frown that Stone still hasn't texted me. I hope that she's okay, but I don't want to hound her so I curl up on the couch and start my mini-marathon of *Buffy*. By noon, I give in and text her again.

Are you okay? I haven't heard from you.

I know she's probably at practice so I don't expect an answer right away. Her Saturdays are packed with either practices or public appearances. It isn't until I finish the first full season that I hear back from her.

I'm fine.

Really? That's all I get? I'm pissed. She is being completely dismissive. I breathe in and out a few times so it won't be my anger answering. *I didn't hear from you last night or today and I thought maybe something happened.* That tells her that I've been thinking of her and I hope she's physically okay and her leg isn't hurting or busted again.

Sorry. Busy. A lot going on.

I put my phone on the coffee table and start season two. I have a feeling I'm in for a long weekend. Something feels off. I don't know if I've pissed her off, how I've pissed her off, or if she's just done with me.

Chapter Thirty-one

I love that we celebrate Halloween at Elite. Tina did an excellent job of decorating the place. The kids are very excited that they're allowed to wear their costumes to PT and trick-or-treat after they're done. All of our employees have candy to hand out and the place is full of excitement. Only I'm not chipper like everybody else. I haven't heard from Stone since that short text message Saturday afternoon. It's been three days. I called her Sunday night, but she didn't answer. I'm not going to beg. I'm an adult and so is she.

"Why didn't you dress up?" Gloria stands in my doorway dressed as a witch, her broom a shiny Swiffer. The green face paint is terrifically scary and her look is topped off with a giant, hairy wart on her cheek.

"More importantly, why didn't you?" I laugh at Gloria's pout. She always goes above and beyond, and this year is no different.

"Most of the kids are your patients. I can't believe you didn't dress up. Are you not feeling well?" That sounds like a good excuse.

"Yeah, I haven't been feeling the greatest all week really." My explanation is lame.

"You're going to have patients who are super excited about today. You know how much kids love dressing up in costumes. I highly recommend you figure something out," she says.

"Agreed. I'm sorry. I'm sure I could find something to wear around here." I'm almost positive we have a janitorial jumpsuit I could put on and come up with some water guns to look like somebody from *Ghostbusters*.

"Your first patient will be here in half of an hour. Go," she says.

I head straight for the closet and find a gray jumpsuit that's too big, but I roll up the legs and sleeves to fit me. I don't have boots, but I do have my running shoes in the car so I grab them. The proton pack is trickier. I find a backpack, a water gun, and some hose. I duct tape the crap out of it until it looks remotely like the weapon used in the movie. By the time my first patient arrives, I've worked up a sweat.

I use a name tag and write the name Holtzmann on it. Two people will get that reference. I look at myself in the mirror. Not bad for a last minute job. I walk into Gloria's office and raise my eyebrows at her. She purses her lips and looks me up and down. I slowly twirl for her.

"The shoes. They throw me off."

"It's all I have except for heels and that's going to look really weird," I say.

"I wish we had slime. That would be fun."

"Says you. Somehow I think I would end up wearing it. Okay, I'm off to work. Get your candy out. Once we're done, we'll bring Davis and Kenna by."

When I head into the room, I smile for the first time in days. Matt is working with Davis this morning, and I'm with my new patient Kenna. She's already informed me that she's going to be a mermaid. Her removable cast is rainbow themed and perfect for a four-year-old. Davis is a cowboy and my little mermaid is adorable.

"What are you supposed to be?" Kenna asks. Of course she isn't going to know who I'm supposed to be. She's four. I'm hopeful Davis saw the movie. I guess I dressed up more for Gloria than my patients.

"I'm supposed to be a ghost catcher." She won't know what a Ghostbuster is, so I explain it in words I think she will understand. I'm not even sure I should have explained that. I wonder if Kenna even knows what a ghost is. If she doesn't, I don't think I should be the one to explain it to her.

"Like Casper? Why would you want to catch him?" Innocence. I love it.

"Well, when Casper doesn't do his exercises, I have to catch him and watch over him to make sure he does," I say. She giggles.

"Casper is friendly and listens to his parents and his doctor," she says, matter-of-factly. She's so clever. I carefully remove her cast and we start working.

She's anxious to finish up and go trick-or-treating so she can show off her mermaid costume. Davis had to take most of his costume off for PT so we wait for him to get dressed. Kenna is wiggling with excitement. I find out that they aren't allowed to wear a costume at her preschool so this is a treat for her. "What kind of candy is there? I like chocolate and gum."

"I guess we'll find out soon enough, huh?" She bounces up and down. I know she wants to tell Davis to hurry, but she doesn't know him so she stands next to me and we wait. Matt helps Davis with his cowboy hat and gun belt. I haven't seen kids this happy in a long time. "Let's go."

Both kids whoop and we walk them around the office, their bags half full by the time we're done. Our routine continues all afternoon. By the end of the day, I'm exhausted but I have a smile on my face. I didn't think about Stone every ten minutes. Because I was busy, I only thought about her every twenty. It was a fun day.

Gloria stops me as I'm getting ready to head out. "Hey, I'm sure you don't want to go home tonight unless you're dying to hand out candy to those hundreds of neighborhood kids. How about going out to dinner with me and Pete?"

I certainly don't want to be the third wheel to their party so I make up something. "Thanks, but I'm going to go see a movie with friends." A movie doesn't sound like a bad idea actually. It's been awhile since I've gone to a theatre and it might be a welcoming distraction.

"Okay, well try to relax a little bit. You still look a little pale."

"Thanks. Have a great dinner. I'll see you in the morning." I peel off my ridiculous outfit and instead of heading home, I pull up a list of movies on my phone. I settle for a science fiction. It doesn't boast of love or romance and it sounds perfectly mindless. I hate that I'm wearing a suit, but I fear going home to change in case the costumed children make their way to my house.

My date for the evening is a tray of junk food and sugary soda. I can't believe that eleven days ago, Stone and I slept together for the first time. A week later, it was our last. A week. I fell for a girl after only a week. I did everything she wanted. We took it relatively slow because she was worried about continuing the pattern of falling into bed with anybody who gave her attention. At this point, I'm upset at myself. Obviously, she doesn't want to talk to me. I've tried several times now and at some point I have to walk away. Our relationship was very new so I can't demand anything really. I need to be an adult about this.

Thankfully, the movie starts and I'm taken from my problems into problems out of this world. Aliens versus people. Stone would like this. No, get out of my head. I take a deep breath and push her out of my mind and force myself to get lost in the movie. Despite my wandering thoughts, I actually start to enjoy the movie. Being alone isn't the worst thing. I'm just happy it's not Valentine's Day. I would be devastated. Luckily, I have plenty of time to recover. I need to get through Thanksgiving and Christmas first, but those are pieces of cake. Both are quick trips to my parents' house, nothing major. It'll be the same as it's always been. I sneak a peek at my phone because I'm strong for only a little bit, but no message. I turn my phone completely off because it's only distracting. I focus hard on the movie. I might as well stay and enjoy it because I just can't go home yet.

Chapter Thirty-two

"Yay, you made it." I grab Rachel and hug her.
"I'm sorry I'm late. I wasn't expecting the meeting to last as long as it did."
"So, come on in." I take her bag. "Make yourself at home."
"This is really a cute place, Hayley," she says.
"Thank you. It has charm and it keeps me hidden from the rest of the world. Or so I thought it did."
She follows me into the kitchen where I pour us wine. "Are you still dealing with Alison?" she asks.
Oh, boy. She doesn't know anything about Stone. "We need to sit down before we have this conversation. Settle in."
Her eyes widen and she grabs the bottle. We get comfortable on the couch. "What is going on? I'm completely on edge over here."
"So, I broke up with Alison, right? Then I started dating a hockey player who was a patient at Elite. We didn't actually start dating until she quit therapy. Yes, it was fast, but it really wasn't a rebound thing for me. I'm not one to jump into a relationship, but there is just something about this woman. Here's the kicker though. We haven't spoken in a week."
She rolls her eyes at me. "A week? Big deal. Sometimes that's normal."
"No, you don't understand. We were really getting along great. I mean, not just the sex, but we were having fun just hanging out. We were talking every day. Something must have happened.

Something big. Just last week she took me on a romantic hayride at her orchard and it was perfect. We both felt something. Then nothing. I texted her a few times and even called her. Not in a stalker kind of way, but just 'how are you doing' type messages."

"Nothing from her at all?" she asks. I shake my head. "What do you think is going on?"

"I don't know. I thought things were good. We were too new to talk about being exclusive so I hope it wasn't because of somebody else. I really thought we had something special."

Rachel reaches over and touches my hand. "I'm sure there's a reason. There has to be. So did you know this hockey player before you left Alison?"

I know she isn't judging me. "I did. She broke some bones. As a favor to her family, Elite agreed to work with her."

"But why you?"

I laugh. "Because Gloria knows I'm really good reasoning with children and I don't get upset very easily. We both know how hard athletes push themselves and Stone's no exception."

"Stone. That's her name? That's very butch."

"That's her last name. Her first name is Elizabeth, but she doesn't like to be called that. She's more of a Stone anyway."

"Are they playing here this weekend?"

"Yes. Right now, tomorrow night, and Sunday afternoon."

"We need to go to the game tomorrow. See what kind of mood she's in. Plus, we can spy and see if she's flirting with anybody," Rachel says.

I roll my eyes even though I know I want to do it. "High school was a long time ago."

She's entirely too excited about this idea and secretly I am, too. "I want to see a hockey game now that I'm in town. There's nothing wrong with that, right?" She sips on her wine and smiles at me over the rim of her glass.

"Most of the games are sold out."

She scoffs at me and pulls out her phone. After several minutes of her typing furiously, she looks at me and smiles. "We have seats in Unity Communications' suite for tomorrow night's game. Pyramid is part of that group."

"No."

"Truth. Here's the kicker. It seats twenty so if you want to invite anybody, we have tickets for three additional people." I know absolutely nobody except for Gloria and some of the other therapists. Since this is a reconnaissance mission, I don't think I should invite the people I'm trying to hide my relationship from.

"Not really, but thanks. Is this a good idea?"

"Of course it is. Then we can observe her and see how she is with anybody else. Spy on her with other players, maybe see if she flirts with any of the fans in the stands." The look on my face must be pretty devastated because she quickly changes the subject. "I'm sure she just has something going on though. Let's talk about something else."

"It's okay. I'm upset by it, but I know that our relationship was very new and I shouldn't be so affected by this, you know? I just was hopeful."

She reaches out and touches my hand. "Look, you're a wonderful woman. Truly. If Stone is going to blow you off like this, then maybe she wasn't the person you thought she was." I'm trying not to cry. I shouldn't be this attached to Stone. I knew it was a mistake to open my heart so soon. I feel like her rebound girl more so than Stone being mine. I can only nod at Rachel. "Let's forget about this and watch something mindless, okay?" She turns on the television and we end up watching a comedy that surprisingly takes my mind off of things.

"Thanks for coming, Rachel. I really need a friend. Most of mine faded away after Alison and I got together. Totally my fault, so I'm glad you're here." She puts a pillow on her lap and tells me to put my head on the pillow. She plays with my hair and I fall asleep within minutes.

❖

"Wow, this place is really exciting. Maybe I should consider dating a hockey player," Rachel says.

I feel like I'm completely exposed. I want to hide in the booth even though I know Stone is in the locker room with her team and can't possibly know that I'm here.

"I'll let you know soon enough if I recommend it or not," I say.

Rachel grabs my hand and drags me up the stairs to the suite. It's impressively large and if I start feeling visible, I can go to the tiny bar inside and pretend to need a drink or some food. We order beers and I grab a plate even though I'm really not hungry. I have to pretend that being this close to Stone and seeing her in just a few minutes isn't tearing me apart inside. I'm actually sweating. I'm in an arena with ice and I feel trickles of sweat at the small of my back and between my shoulder blades. Thankfully, I'm wearing a sweater that hides my nervousness.

Because Rachel is so fashionable, I had to step up my game and dress a bit nicer than I did the last time I was here. I settled on a pair of black slacks and a charcoal sweater with a white oxford underneath. Rachel loans me a necklace that matches my outfit well. She even fixed my hair. We both look great. A part of me wants to run into Stone tonight, but maybe after I get a better idea of what's happening.

"This is great. I've never been to a hockey game before." Rachel stands next to me and we soak it all in.

"Do you know anything about hockey at all?" I ask.

"Not a damn thing. You'll have to tell me what's going on."

I almost laugh. I've found another lesbian who knows nothing about the sport. It's too bad I can't tell Stone that I'm not the only one. "I know there are three periods and that makes the game longer than I like. I know Stone's a forward so she has the opportunity to score a lot. And I know that the goalie protects the net."

"Oh, so it's like soccer. That's easy enough," she says.

"You know more than I do, trust me." I really do need to learn both sports. If someone like Rachel knows more about sports than

I do, then I should abandon all extra-curricular activities and only study sports. Hell, I was even a therapist to athletes. I have no excuse.

Rachel smiles at me and shakes her head. "Let's grab a seat. The lights are getting crazy. Things are starting."

The crowd's already yelling and screaming, anxious for the Gray Wolves to take to the ice. The cheerleaders form lines on either side of the entrance to the rink and each home player is introduced. When Stone skates out, the entire stadium roars. I can't help but smile even though I don't want to.

"That's her, right?" I nod. We both watch her zip around the rink. "She's really fast." She points to Stone's picture in the program. "And really cute." I can only nod. Seeing Stone so close, yet so far away really hurts. More than I thought. "And really tall." She's at least four or five inches taller than the rest of the team. They line up when a little girl sings a heartfelt rendition of the national anthem. I can't keep my eyes off Stone. She looks hard, fierce, and ready to kill. Her jaw is clenched and her eyes bright and focused. "Scratch that to really pretty," Rachel says after the crowd cheers the little singer.

We sit down when the game starts. The Gray Wolves fall back on defense immediately. I can tell Stone is more comfortable with skating. She fouls within the first few minutes. And checks a few players. The coach pulls her out and she hits her stick on the side of the bench before she sits down.

"She's not happy about something." I don't realize I said it out loud until Rachel responds.

"See? Maybe something is happening with her. If she's already moved on, she wouldn't be this angry. She would be fun and flirty, not aggressive and pissed off. We should stick around after the game to see what happens."

I shrug indifferently. At least Rachel doesn't call my bullshit. She turns back to the ice and watches the game. I'm concentrating on Stone. I can't see her face from this angle, but her body language speaks volumes. She's not sitting close to the team, and she only has eyes for the game. I'm sad for her. I want to reach out and smooth the hard line on her forehead that I know is there without even seeing her face.

My phone buzzes in my pocket. It's Alison. *What are you doing tomorrow?*

I don't feel anxious anymore when she reaches out to me. Just annoyed.

I have a friend in from out of town until tomorrow. She doesn't need to know anything else about Rachel. Let her think what she wants.

Can we do a late lunch or early dinner? Since we'll be working together, I think it might be a good idea to bury the hatchet and try to be friends.

That actually sounds like an okay idea. I'm still a little skeptical, but she does have a point. I know Gloria's going to need me to help more so I agree on an early dinner. We decide to meet at a soup and sandwich shop downtown, a place neither of us has been to before. Neutral territory.

"Who was that?" Rachel sits next to me after getting us each another beer.

"Alison. She wants to do an early dinner to try to figure out how to get along since we're going to be working together for the Holiday fund-raiser."

Rachel raises her eyebrows at me. "Are you okay with that?"

I shrug. "I think. Our paths will cross from time to time so we're going to have to start somewhere."

"Okay. If you want, I can hang around and go with you. Then we'll know if she's in it for friendship or more."

"Thanks, but I think I can handle it. I do appreciate the thought, but you can't babysit me during our fundraising meetings over the next month or so."

"That makes me sad, but I agree. Just stay strong, okay? I know you aren't going to get back with her, but just tread carefully, you know what I mean?" She reaches over and squeezes my knee in a reassuring way.

"I promise. I like myself too much right now to get lost again. Even if I'm a little sad about Stone."

She puts her arm around my shoulders. "Hey, we're here to cheer you up. I saw cake up there. I think we both deserve a piece." We still have time before the third period starts so I follow her to the buffet table where they are serving coffee, brownies, cake, and freshly baked cookies.

"This is fantastic. I'm so happy your parent company has a suite. I should see all the games from here." The pampering we've received has been top notch.

"Any time you want to come back, I'll make a call."

We spend a few minutes talking with other guests in the suite before the start of the final period. The closer we get to the end of the game, the faster my heart beats and the sweatier my palms become. I don't think we'll see Stone after the game even though a part of me hopes that we do. The Gray Wolves take the ice and I lean forward when I see Stone. The crowd cheers as they make a final circle around the ice before taking the bench. Stone waves to the crowd, a huge smile on her face. The box we're in is close enough to the ice for me to make out Stone's features. Her smile doesn't reach her eyes. Nobody else knows that though. She looks up and I know she sees me. I can feel it. For the briefest of moments, our eyes connect and I feel heat, passion, and sadness.

"Did she just see you?" Rachel turns to me.

I nod. "I think so. What should I do?"

"Watch the game. Then go home. If she calls or texts you, then you know she saw you for sure and wants to be with you." Rachel is too optimistic.

"What if she doesn't?"

She reaches out for my hand. "Then you know it wasn't meant to be. We'll binge on ice cream and bad television, okay?"

Stone starts the final period and she's on fire. Within the first minute, she scores. I see her look up our way and I swear that point was for me. Maybe I'm reading too much into it, but it makes me feel good, even if only for a second. She scores another goal within three minutes and looks at the box again. This time Rachel notices.

"If she doesn't call you tonight, I'll be incredibly shocked," she says. I don't say it, but I will be, too. "If you want to, we can stay."

"No. You're right. She knows I'm here. She can make the next move." I stand and nod my head toward the door. Rachel smiles and follows me.

"Now that is a definite statement. And I'm proud of you." She locks her arm with mine and we head out early to beat the crowd. "I still don't know if I should date a hockey player," she says.

"I'll let you know tomorrow if it's worth it."

Chapter Thirty-three

"Thanks for meeting me." Alison gives me a quick, albeit awkward hug and we grab a booth close to the window.
"No problem. You look good," I say. She does.
"You look a little tired today." I can tell she's not being mean. "Did you have fun with your friend this weekend?" she asks.
"Yeah, we stayed up too late last night and the night before. She's the girl I met in New York that one weekend." I regret saying that because it brings up a time when we were together, but I don't want Alison to get the wrong idea. I know I look bad. I only slept a few hours. Stone never called, she never texted. I'm completely spent. I threw in the towel this morning. Rachel was very kind and supportive and promised to hate hockey for the rest of her life when she left this morning. I'm going to visit her next month and we're going on a shopping spree in the big city.
"So, other than being tired, how have you been? How are your parents?"
"I'm good. I've been staying busy at work. I have a few infants now as patients," I say.
"That's great news. It's what you've always wanted." She seems so sincere that it's easy to fall into a rhythm with her. We order a light dinner. She orders bread and a salad with creamy dressing on it. She rarely indulges. I don't hold back and order the club sandwich with broccoli and cheese soup. It's yummy and I savor every bite. I didn't think I had an appetite.

"My parents are doing well, too. Dad got a new car. They've just been doing normal, boring parent stuff. They are healthy and happy so that's all that matters."

"Agreed. I'm glad they're well."

Now that all of the niceties are done, I want to get down to business. "Now that we know the who, what, when, and where for the fund-raiser, we have to figure out the how. Does Regional have any decorations? I know we do, but they are all cartoony. Wait. Do we even have money in the budget for decorations?"

"I'm sure we can work something out with someone. People aren't usually jerks to hospitals and will work with us," she says confidently.

"People know hospitals have money. They might double the bill."

She laughs. "You're probably right. We can make a list of things with Gloria on Thursday and see if she has any ideas. She's done this a ton of times."

"That's true. This is what she wants to do. That's why she gave me her patients. She likes to do the behind the scenes stuff at Elite. I'm glad because I'd much rather deal with the patients," I say.

Alison orders us both small pieces of cake. I pretend to not want it for about three seconds, then greedily take the plate.

"Thanks for meeting me, Hayley. I appreciate it. I know I probably seemed a little crazy showing up at your door a few weeks ago and I'm sorry for that," she says.

"I'm sorry I was a jerk. I really was busy that night." I don't feel the need to explain Stone, especially to Alison so I let it drop. Surprisingly, she doesn't push for more information. I figured she'd be dying to know why a famous athlete showed up to collect me. I don't ask her how she knew how to find me. I just don't care anymore.

❖

Gloria sits down with a steaming cup of coffee. "You met with Alison yesterday? How did that go?" It's eight thirty Monday morning. She doles out the chocolate croissants she bought for us and we have a quick breakfast in my office. Coffee with her from eight thirty to eight forty five has become a daily ritual. The croissants are a new twist.

"She was fine actually. Didn't act needy or possessive. By the end of dinner, I felt like I just had dinner with a friend. Nothing more."

Gloria raises her eyes at me. "Really?"

"She didn't pump me for information on my life. Alison has heard about me spending time with two different women. I don't know if I would have been so quiet if the roles were reversed."

"Back up. You're dating two different women right now? How do I not know about this? I thought I was your best friend."

Well, now I'm going to have to come up with something and I hate lying, but I'm still a chicken shit and not ready to tell her the truth. Besides, if Stone and I are over, what's the sense in telling her? "I'm not dating anybody right now." This is true. "I told you about Rachel, the girl I met in the city when I went to New York with my parents? She came into town this past weekend and the other was also just a friend." Okay, that part is a small lie, but only partly. Stone was my friend at the time, not officially a girlfriend, but more of a friend with benefits. I can justify a lot in my mind.

"So you're at least somewhat comfortable with Alison and coming to all of our meetings now, right?"

"Yes, but please don't make me the lead."

"Oh, Hayley. I would never do that to you. We'll do the meeting Thursday and then you probably won't see her until we have to decorate for the event. Does this mean you won't have a date? Because there is a very cute and very single lesbian who works in Pete's office that I think you might be interested in."

I hold up my hand to stop her. "No. No, you don't. I'm a big girl and I can find my own dates, but thank you for thinking of me." Suddenly, we're in a staring contest. She should know better. She sighs and looks away first. "I win."

She busts out laughing and stands up. "There is a reason why you work so well with children. You're nothing but a child yourself."

"One of us is a sore loser today."

She nods and shrugs. "What can I say? It's Monday. Get back to work."

"Hey, Gloria?" She turns back from the doorway. "Thanks for breakfast and for always being a good friend."

Chapter Thirty-four

Stone's car is already in the practice arena parking lot along with two others. It's six forty-five and I'm sitting in my car like a stalker, debating if I should go inside or not. What if the door is locked? She's not going to be okay with me coming in, but I can't stand this anymore. I need to know what happened. I take a deep breath and get out of my car. By the time I reach the door, my entire body feels heavy. I don't want to know the truth, but I have to hear it directly from her.

As quietly as I can, I open the door and slip inside. My heart tumbles and I have to grab the handrail when I see her. I don't think I'm ready for this. My body is instantly hot. I unbutton my coat. I'm not good at confrontations, but the new me, the new and improved Hayley Sims, is going to confront my problems and issues head on, starting with Stone. I slip into the back near the bleachers and watch as Stone trains. She is as intense as ever. The dragon is on the ice today, just like she was last Saturday. I'm not worried about her leg, I'm worried about her demeanor. She is all sorts of angry and now I'm second guessing my decision. I should discreetly make my way to the door and slip out like I wasn't even here.

Someone steps into my sightline. "What are you doing in here? You can't be in here." Great. I'm being accosted by the custodian slash Zamboni driver. I quickly look over at Stone, but it's too late. She sees us. So much for my inconspicuous exit.

"I'm here to see Stone," I say.

He turns to Stone. "Are you expecting someone?"

She stares at me for a few seconds. "It's okay, Joe. Thanks for looking out. I should have mentioned somebody was dropping by." She waits until he's far enough away before she says anything. "What are you doing here, Doc?"

Her guard is up. It's going to be hard to get through to her. I stand firm. "I need to know why you blew me off. I'm not trying to act clingy, but you at least owe me an explanation. Especially after everything." I emphasize that word. My fingernails dig into my palms. I stand there and wait. She answers me with a shrug. "Really? After everything, that's what I get? A shrug? You told me you wanted this. You wanted a lasting relationship, something longer than one night. I wouldn't have invested time or my heart into you."

Her expression wavers, but only for a moment. "Look, H— Doc. Some things just aren't meant to be. This is a good time to move on for both of us. The season is hard because I'm gone every weekend and my practices are late so it just doesn't make sense to start something." Her eyes soften, at least I think. She looks down at her skates, then adjusts them.

"Start something? Are you serious? I'm pretty sure we already started something. Maybe it's different in your world, but once I sleep with somebody, I tend to be invested. Physically and emotionally. If you didn't want this, us, you should have said something. Called me or stopped by just to cut it off completely instead of leaving me hanging." I'm starting to tremble. That means I'm only a few minutes away from losing my shit and crying. She finally looks at me.

"You need somebody who can be there for you. I'm just not that person. I'm sorry if I led you on, but this is what's best for both of us," she says almost nonchalantly.

"I'm so pissed at you. You don't know what's best for me."

"I might not know, but Alison said—" she stops talking.

"Wait. What did you just say? Have you been talking to Alison? Behind my back?" I move so I'm directly in front of her. "What is going on?"

"I know this sounds shitty, but Alison and I talked a few weeks ago. Everything she said made sense. I agree with her. I can't give you what she or somebody who has a normal life can. At least not now," she says.

"Are you fucking kidding me? Let me get this straight. You and my ex-fiancée got together to determine who gets me? What did you do? Flip a coin or something? Do my feelings not count for anything?" I'm livid. I'm one step away from screaming or throwing something. I don't think I've ever been this angry.

"Hayley, calm down. It wasn't like that."

"You'd better start explaining yourself."

She takes a deep breath. "Alison came to a game a few weeks ago and waited for me out in the parking lot. She pointed out all the reasons you shouldn't be with me and they all made sense. You deserve someone who can be there for you all of the time. I'm gone five months out of the year. It's not fair to you."

I point at her. "You do not get to decide what's best for me. The only thing you get to do is decide if you want to date me or not date me, but it needs to be your decision, not somebody else's. Do you know how hard this has been for me?"

"I'm sorry. I really am. I never meant to hurt you," she says.

I stare at her for a long time. "So that's it? Alison decides and you go along with it? That doesn't sound like you at all. That's weak. And a cop out. Just say it. I want to hear it come from you. Tell me you don't want to be with me. Tell me you don't want us." I brush away my tears. I don't even care that I'm crying in front of her. I want her to see what this decision has done to me. I want her to know how hurt I am.

"It's just better this way." She turns and skates away.

I haven't been this embarrassed and angry in a long time. I make it out to my car before I completely melt down. I head back to my house to splash water on my face and reapply my makeup.

My day's just beginning. I have lunch later with Alison and Gloria and I plan on unleashing on Alison. Nobody gets to play with my heart. I stare at myself a long time. My eyes are slightly bloodshot, but the blotchiness on my face is gone. I'm done letting other people decide what's best for me. I'm done getting my heart torn to pieces. From now on, my life and my emotions are mine to protect at all costs. I'm not doing this again. Next time, I won't be so free with my heart.

❖

"Hey, Gloria, now that we are done, can you give us a minute?" Our meeting just ended. A lot of decisions were made and now we have a plan. Gloria was right. Alison and I won't have any more contact until the actual event.

"Of course." Gloria catches my eye before she leaves the room. I nod to let her know it's okay.

"What's up?" Alison asks. She leans back in her chair and looks relaxed and happy. That's about to change.

"Here's what I'm trying to figure out. I know you want to be friends, but how do you expect me to be happy and upbeat when I know you approached Stone and told her to stay away from me? Tell me how we're supposed to be friends after you do something like that?" I stand up and lean over the table. I can feel my face flush with anger. Her face is the exact opposite of mine. She's pale and visibly distraught.

"I just want what's best for you, Hayley. Please try to understand that." She reaches out to me.

I recoil. "Why does every single person in my life think they know what is best for me? I, Hayley Sims, know what's best for me. Not you, not Stone. Not anyone. So here's what's going to happen. I'm going to date who I want, when I want, and you're not going to get involved. The days of you dictating everything about me are over. Remember that. Stay out of my life, Alison."

I storm out of the conference room. Alison can find her own way out. I slam the door to my office and sit on the couch. I need to settle down. My one o'clock is going to be here in a few minutes and I can't be worked up. Babies sense stress and I need to make sure it's out of my body. I shake my limbs and take several long, deep breaths. I will the negativity to leave my body. Even though my heart hurts at my loss, I feel one hundred times better after confronting both Stone and Alison. At least I know. I'm not what Stone wants, but now I can close that chapter in my life.

Chapter Thirty-five

"Honey, are you coming Wednesday night or Thursday morning? I need to know when to get your room ready." Thanksgiving is this week and my mother has been pressuring me to give her an answer.

"I'll head down Thursday morning. Do you need me to bring anything?" I know my mom ordered everything in advance, but it's still nice to offer.

"No, we're fine. Just yourself. We'll see you by noon, okay?" I guess I should be happy I don't have to worry about baking something, but I hate showing up empty-handed. I could go up to the orchard and pick out some apples for a pie, but I have a fear of running into Stone. If I go when I know she's at practice, our paths shouldn't cross. And those pies I made were delicious. Even if my mom is on one of her crazy diets, my dad will appreciate it. I decide to check my ingredients. I only need apples. I look up the orchard's holiday schedule and find that they're closing early tomorrow so I should probably get up there now. I grab my keys and head out, trying not to second guess my decision. Stone won't be there. She's at practice. I find myself repeating that, yet I'm still disappointed when I don't see her SUV in the parking lot.

It's crowded because of the holiday, but I know exactly what I want. I grab a basket and pick the same three kinds of apples as I used before. A very attractive and very tall woman motions me to her register when I'm next in line.

"Did you find everything you were looking for?" she asks. I thank her and nod, anxious to get out of here. "Here's your card back, Ms. Sims. Oh, wait. Are you Elizabeth's therapist? The one who made the apple pie? It was so good."

For fuck's sake. I really didn't want this to happen either. I wanted Brian to check me out like he did before so I could go home unscathed, undetected, and completely miserable.

"Yes. Hi, I'm Hayley. I'm glad you liked the pie. I absolutely adore your orchard." Panic sets in as she stares at me with her sapphire eyes. They aren't as bright as Stone's, but just as intense. What does her mother know about me? About us?

"Thank you. You did a remarkable job with her. She came home after the first day raving about you. You put her in her place and earned her respect from the very beginning," she says.

"I'm glad she's back on the ice and doing well."

"She's so happy to be back doing what she loves. We owe you so much."

I'm pretty sure at this point she doesn't know about us so I breathe a sigh of relief. "Thank you, but I really enjoy working with patients and getting them back doing what they love. Stone was a good patient." Her mom rolls her eyes at me. I laugh. "Seriously, she did everything right and I have no complaints." Except for the whole let's fuck and never talk again thing.

"If you stick around a few more minutes, she should be here," she says.

My whole body forgets how to move. I fumble around trying to gather my stuff so I can get the hell out of there. Why doesn't Stone have practice tonight? The door seems so far away and Stone's really nice mother is in no hurry to end this conversation even though the line to check out is getting longer and longer.

"As much as I'd love to see her, I really need to get home and bake pies for Thanksgiving. I have a full day tomorrow and then I'm off to see my parents." Why am I telling this woman my life story?

"Of course. I'll tell Elizabeth you said hello."

I wish she wouldn't. I head out the door and double time it to my car. I pull out of the parking lot right when Stone pulls in. She looks confused. I break eye contact to turn into traffic when it clears. Even though I start to shake, I'm proud of myself for being able to leave without showing any emotion when our eyes met.

❖

The drive to my parents' house is peaceful. I listen to soundtracks and sing at the top of my lungs. By the time I pull into the driveway, I'm ready for a nap. My mother won't allow it and puts me to work in the kitchen. We all know the meal is pre-made, but she wants to serve it in her dishes. I think it's a waste of clean plates and servers, but she's all about making it look nice. Truthfully, my father would be okay with a pizza. It's hard to be traditional when your family consists of only three people. The last few years, Alison at least helped even out the numbers.

"What's Alison doing this holiday?" My mother doesn't waste time. Dad shoots Mom a look. Apparently, she's not as concerned about my feelings as he is. I shrug at her. I honestly don't know if they have stayed in contact.

"I don't know. She didn't clue me in the last time we talked." I sound bitchy.

"She's probably working at the hospital now that…" Mom's voice trails off. "You know what I mean."

"Well, one day soon she'll find someone and then we won't have to worry about her." I really need to snap out of this mood. My parents have always cared about Alison. I know it's hard for them to move on. They're still working through the break up.

"We're still adjusting, honey. She's a nice girl and we want to make sure she isn't alone during the holidays," my dad says.

"I know. I'm sorry I'm being such an ass about it all." I won't tell them about Alison trying to control my life even after being out of it for some time now. I don't want to have to explain why I got into another relationship so quickly, and I don't want to explain why it ended just as fast.

Seeing Stone in the parking lot was harder than I thought. I'm glad I'm away for the next few days even if I will be bored stiff. I purposely left my phone in the car. I don't want to stare at my phone the entire time I'm here, waiting for her to reach out to me.

Our early dinner is perfect because we eat, clean up, and nap. This life is simple. I read while my dad watches the football games. My mom knits for a bit, then organizes photos. Tomorrow will be a different story. We'll get up early and shop, then I'll head home. One night with my parents is about all I can stand. I get why Stone was going stir crazy at the orchard. As emotionally chaotic as my life is, it's still mine and I already miss it. Plus, it's hard to wallow in self-pity when my mom is watching me like a hawk. I think she's waiting for me to fall apart so she can swoop in and save me. Little does she know that if I do, it won't be because of Alison, but because of a certain tall, blue-eyed hockey player who has gotten under my skin and into my heart.

Chapter Thirty-six

Gloria pops her head into my office before heading out to an off-site meeting. "We have a field trip Friday afternoon so don't even think of making plans."

"What's going on?" I ask.

"I can't tell you. That would ruin all of the fun. Dress warm and casually. We're taking the bus out," She quickly exits my office.

We rarely do field trips, but when we do, it's usually for the children. Gloria must have arranged the trip with all of my afternoon patients or rescheduled them. I'm intrigued. I call Matt, but he either doesn't know, or is keeping his mouth shut. I shrug. It's not as if I have plans Friday night so getting out of the office sounds like fun. My life has been a complete bore. I've promised myself that at the start of the new year, I'm going to go online and sign up for a dating site. At least online I can be choosy and somewhat discreet. It's too bad Rachel lives so far away. Not that we would date, but she has a ton of friends she could set me up with and she could take me to places to meet potential girlfriends. Three years is a long time to be out of the dating pool.

"Baby Ava is here," Tina announces.

No matter what my mood is, knowing that a happy baby is waiting to play with me, puts a smile on my face. I'll be able to easily forget my problems for the next forty-five minutes. Ava's doing remarkably well, eager to please me and her parents. I have complete faith that she'll catch up to the other babies in no time. Now that I have PT with two infants, the desire to have a family is starting to pull at me a little. At this point, I'd be okay having a child on my own. I have a great job, an understanding boss, and I could easily bring my baby to work if I had to. Gloria has made it clear that even though she doesn't take care of patients, she is more than willing to take care of babies. Ava makes all sorts of noises when I walk into the room. She's not talking yet, but she sure has a lot to babble about.

"Your boss said Matt's going to work with Ava on Friday," Marti says.

I try to not show my surprise. "We have a field trip Friday afternoon. I trust Matt with my patients. He's very good and we are in constant communication. He's great with babies, too." I call him over to meet the Sullivans so their minds are put at ease. Charming as always, he wins them over in no time, including Ava who happily reaches out to him.

"She's improved so much not only with her PT, but socially as well. Thank you so much for all that you've done," Marti says.

"This is all her. She's at the pivotal age where she's starting to understand things better so she wants to participate more." Of course, if they want me to take the credit, I totally will. "In a few months, she won't need Elite. She'll be on her own, walking and running around with the rest of the toddlers."

"We can only hope. Have fun on your field trip Friday and we'll see you next week." Marti dances out the door with Ava who is happily squealing. I'm sad I won't see her until next week.

"I can't wait until I get to work with babies, too," Matt says.

I feel guilty for taking the infants, but with seniority, I automatically get them if my schedule allows. "I think the next infant we get as a patient, you get to work with him or her."

The smile on his face couldn't be any bigger. "That would be great. Thanks. And I promise to take extra care of Ava Friday while you're doing whatever you're off doing."

I shrug again. As much as I'm trying not to think about Friday, my curiosity is definitely piqued.

❖

I pull out my favorite sweater and slip it on over my turtleneck. Gloria told me to dress warmly and casually. I'll probably roast in the office, but at least I won't be cold during our secret getaway this afternoon. I pour my second cup of coffee and head out. I want to get this day done. I'm looking forward to my weekend of online Christmas shopping and excessive napping. We haven't seen snow yet, but I know it's coming soon. I probably should invest in snow removal equipment or get to know my neighbors better and find a teenager who is willing to shovel when the time comes.

"Are you ready for some fun?" Gloria unlocks the door for me. She never beats me in. I look at my watch to make sure I'm not late.

"What are you doing here so early?"

She stands back so I can slip past her. "I want to get this day started. Breakfast is in my office today."

"Okay, let me put my stuff away and I'll be there in a second." I set my messenger bag on the couch and turn on my computer to check my emails. I've stopped looking for personal emails from Stone. At least not first thing.

Gloria peeks into my office. "Bring your coffee cup."

"Say it isn't so." I stand up when she nods. I grab my cup and follow her to the corner office where a brand new Keurig sits on her credenza. "It's beautiful. Let's break it in."

She opens the drawer where there are several boxes of different flavors of coffee. "I'm pretty sure I owe you all of these."

"Stop. You do enough for me. Nobody's keeping tabs." I make a cup of medium roast and sit on the couch next to her.

"I still owe you a nice dinner and some fancy chocolates or something ridiculous like that," she says.

"What are you talking about?" I laugh.

"For taking Stone as a patient. You said I had to take you out and spend a lot of money on you." Nice moment gone.

I keep a smile pasted on my face though. I'm trying to get better at forgetting Stone, but it's hard when I'm not expecting her to be mentioned by others around me. "Stop. Not at all. I was just doing my job."

"Well, I understand she's kicking ass at hockey so you did everything I asked you to do. So pick a night and we'll go out. Oh, and get this. Stone Orchard is donating five thousand dollars to the Holiday fund-raiser event."

"Shut up. Are you serious?" I'm in shock. "That's fantastic." I wonder if Stone had anything to do with that donation or if she even knows about it.

"That's all because of you. You did more for Stone than I did. I'm sure she and her parents are forever in debt to you and us."

"I'm just happy she's doing as well as she is. I had faith in her, but her comeback was all determination and hustle. I was just there showing her the ropes." I really want to change the subject. I notice a white pastry bag on her desk. "Is that what I think it is?" I point to it and smile at her.

"Cinnamon donuts fresh from Lamont's Bakery."

"I'm so in love with you right now." I follow her to the desk and wait for her to dole them out. She digs up napkins and offers me the bag first. I take a fresh, still warm donut from the top. "You know, I was losing weight there for awhile, but this decadence a few times a week is starting to add up." That doesn't stop me from taking a giant bite. I moan in culinary appreciation.

"Best donuts in town."

"Best donuts in the world," I say. We eat in silence. Sort of. There's a lot of lip smacking and soft moans. If anybody were to hear us, they would think we were making out. "So are you going to tell me what we're doing this afternoon?"

"Absolutely not. I'm glad you are dressed appropriately."

This is the first time we are doing a winter field trip. Most of our trips are spring and summer. The small bus we have is used to pick up patients who otherwise wouldn't have a ride to Elite. Tom, our bus driver, stays pretty busy most days. He's a giant man with an even bigger heart. It'll be fun to see how the kids take to him.

"Who all is going on this trip?" That seems like an easy enough question that won't reveal too much.

"Most of your patients, a few of Matt's. And a few parents to help us out. Now quit asking questions and let's eat another donut." I reach out before she even gets the last word out. I agree. Today should just be brainless and fun. "So this morning just get your paperwork caught up and we'll meet at noon in the lobby." We end up talking for half an hour before the rest of the employees start trickling in. That's my cue. I stand to head back to my office.

"Thanks for the donuts and coffee. Congrats on the beautiful coffee maker. I'm jealous now."

"What's mine is yours. And we're still going to do dinner. Pick a night next week, and I'll pick the place." I shake my head at her, then nod. No use arguing with the boss.

Chapter Thirty-seven

Gloria calls my office phone from the parking lot. "There aren't enough seats on the bus. Do you mind driving separately?" The bus seats fourteen and there are fifteen of us.

"No sweat, but now you have to tell me where we're going." I can't stop from smiling.

"Nice try. Can you follow us?" I hear the stress in her voice and it makes me sober up.

"No problem. Let me grab my stuff and I'll be in the lobby in a few seconds." I shut off my computer and grab my keys and my bag. I doubt I'll be back this evening and that makes me even happier. I show up just as the last parent steps onto the bus.

"Why's everybody early?" I look down at my watch. We aren't even supposed to meet for another four minutes.

"I think everybody's just excited about today. Are you ready?" Gloria asks.

"Sure. I'll follow you." I'm not about to mess with her. I can tell she's still flustered. "Don't worry about a thing." She gives me a quick one arm hug and hops on the bus. I hustle to my car and pull up behind them. Even if I don't know where I'm going, it's going to be hard to lose the green and blue bus. Plus, I can always call Gloria. I turn down the radio so I can concentrate and follow.

After about ten minutes, my palms start sweating. This can't be happening. We take the exit I don't want to take. We pull into the parking lot I don't want to pull into. I park beside the bus and stare at the Bushnell Arena, the arena where the Gray Wolves play. This has Stone written all over it. There's a knock at my window and I jump.

"Come on, Hayley. We've got children to corral." Gloria opens the door for me. I sigh and step out of my car, my anxiety bubbling up and threatening to spill out.

"So this is the surprise?" I ask.

"Sort of. Come on." We head toward the entrance, Gloria leading the pack, me at the rear. I'd love to sneak away, but even with some parents helping, we're lacking numbers. I have to stick around. We walk into a dim arena. Gloria points at a roped off area in the seats and we all sit down and wait. As much as I don't want to see Stone, I'm starting to feel the excitement. The kids are smiling and happy. It's hard not to get caught up in the moment.

"Ladies and gentlemen. Are you ready for some fun?" We hear over the loudspeaker. Color lights flash and bob around the ice and the kids start yelling and screaming. When the Gray Wolves' mascot takes the ice, they get louder and jump up and down. The mascot skates over to the kids and leans over the railing to high five them. He skates to a box on the ice and slides it to the kids. Inside are all Gray Wolves' jerseys personalized for the kids and even the parents. I can feel my eyes sting with tears. All of this must have cost Stone and the team a fortune. I remember when Stone told me how much she admired these kids. Gloria hands me my jersey and sits down next to me. Instead of Sims, mine reads Doc.

"Stone wanted to do this as a surprise for you and your patients," she says. I almost cry right there. The jersey is too small to fit over my sweater so I take it off and put the jersey over my turtleneck.

"This is perfect," I say and quickly add, "for the kids."

"Oh, this is only the beginning," she says. The lights dim down again and the loudspeaker announces some of the players. The kids go wild when Stone skates out. The music dies down and Stone and four other players skate over to us. I can't make eye contact with her.

"Who here wants to play hockey?" Stone asks. Every single kid raises their hand.

"Parents and docs, go get fitted for skates if you want to come out on the ice. The kids get a special treat. We are going to use those." She points to the mascot who returns with three ice sleds.

"I'll sit back here with the parents who don't want to get out on the ice. I hope you go out there," Gloria says. I turn to her. I'm not going out on the ice. I haven't skated in years. "Go on. Go get fitted for skates. I'll watch our stuff." I can't say no to her. I'm sure she thinks everything's great with Stone and I'm just as excited about this as the kids are when, in reality, I want to sneak out the back door and run away to Alaska.

"I don't really need to be out there, do I?" I hate that I already know the answer.

I sigh and follow one of the players who is taking some parents over to the practice rink to be fitted for skates. Thank God I'm wearing thick socks. I remember always needing the padding around my ankles on roller blades and ice skates. The attendant hands me a pair of size eight skates and tells me to make sure they're snug enough. I head back to the other rink, dreading the thought of having to spend time with Stone. Just when she wasn't always on my mind.

Gloria applauds me as I make my way onto the ice. Stone and two of the other Gray Wolves are carefully pulling children around on the sleds. Their smiles couldn't be any bigger. Each sled has a hockey stick and the kids take turns trying to hit the pucks. The children who can't use the sticks are riding shotgun in the sleds. Every single person is having a great time except me. I carefully step onto the ice, avoiding all eye contact. I plan on staying in the back until somebody needs me.

"Doc, come on over here." I look up and for the first time, make eye contact with Stone. Her eyes are warm and her smile is hesitant, but genuine. It's hard not to smile when all of the kids are looking at Stone like she's their hero.

"I'm not great at skating."

She crooks her finger at me. I hate that she's so charming. I'm mad at her. I'm angry that she can act so cavalier. She broke my heart weeks ago and now she's acting like we didn't have sex ten different ways or share tenderness. Hell, I even cried the first time we slept together. No, now she's playful and fun and it's as if the relationship between us is a happy one. I almost slip down the side of the wall I'm leaning on when she heads my way, her eyes steady on me. She stands a foot from me. I have to look up at her.

"Come on. Let's put aside our differences for these kids, okay? I want them to have a good time. Show them that you aren't afraid."

"You understand that I'm completely pissed at you and if it wasn't for my boss and these kids, I would have never pulled into the parking lot." I deliver this with a fake smile.

"Yeah, I told Gloria you probably wouldn't want to attend if you knew. I know you aren't going to like this, but I had to confess to her."

"What? You told Gloria about us?" I'm embarrassed and even more upset.

"We can talk about it later, but yes, in a roundabout way," Stone says.

"We can't talk about it later. Now I've got to do damage control and pray that I don't lose my job. How could you? I was ready to forget about all of this and pretend we didn't even happen." I know my voice is getting loud. She reaches out and gently holds my upper arms.

"Please, Hayley. I have a lot to say and I know now isn't the time. Let's put that on hold just for a little bit. Can we please talk later? I promise I won't blow you off and be an ass. Again," she says. I look into her blue eyes and I know she's telling the truth. She's vulnerable. My icy walls crack a bit. I nod curtly. She gives my arms a quick squeeze and skates away. "Okay, Davis, apparently Miss Hayley needs some encouragement. Want to help get her?" He nods and Stone pulls the sled around and heads my way. I swallow my ego, my heart, my feelings, and push off the wall to meet them halfway.

"Miss Hayley, you can skate." He sounds disappointed that he isn't coming to my rescue after all.

"I still need your help, Davis. I haven't skated in a long time. If you stay near me, I can reach out to you if I start to fall." I'm actually impressed with myself. Even though my skates are tight and already rubbing against my ankles, skating feels pretty good. This makes me appreciate Stone and her desire to be back on the ice even more. Davis high fives me and I almost fall. I quickly grab onto the sled. "See? I told you I needed you." He laughs and Stone chuckles. I still can't look at her. I'm having a hard time keeping my emotions in check. I wish Gloria would've told me what we were doing today. I could've emotionally prepared myself. Of course, I probably would have figured out a way to get out of this trip. Now that Gloria knows the history, I'm surprised she was okay with it. I should be mad at her, but I feel like I owe her an apology, too. This whole thing is fucked up. Thank God it's Friday and I can hide for the next two days of my life. I just need to get through the next two hours.

I take a moment to skate over to Brittney and Kenna who are sharing a sled. It's their turn to hit pucks. Emily, the Gray Wolves' starting goalie, is carefully pulling their sled. She pulls them closer and closer to the goal. Stone skates over to play goalie while the girls take shots. The first few attempts, Stone blocks and everybody boos her. On the fourth one, she dives well in advance of the shot and the goal is wide open. Brittney steadies the stick and gently knocks the puck in. Our entire group screams and yells. The smile on her face couldn't be bigger. I can't help but applaud and celebrate, too. As much as I want to dislike Stone right now, it's really hard. This is so good for the kids' morale and their healing process. Today is Stone's way of telling them that they can do anything they want to.

The loudspeaker announces lunch and everybody heads back to the seats. The second level has opened up a kiosk where they are offering hot dogs, hamburgers, fries, pretzels, ice cream, and soda. I'm starving so I head up there and grab a plate.

I sit down with Brittney and congratulate her again on her goal. I'm so happy the kids are talkative because I really don't have a lot to say. My emotions are physically draining. This is so much easier. Let them talk and I can sit back and not think about things. It's hard when Stone's this close though. She is two tables away being worshipped by the kids and their parents.

After lunch, it's going to be the parents and the Gray Wolves playing a little exhibition game. I draw the line there. I will not be a participant, I will only be a spectator. There will be two Gray Wolves and three parents on each team. Gloria, the kids, and I are going to be the cheerleaders eating popcorn and yelling with our mouths full. Even though I'm only here because I was tricked, I'm actually having fun. But it's only a matter of time before I have to have serious talks with both Gloria and Stone and that puts a damper on my mood.

Chapter Thirty-eight

"At some point, we should talk." I slide next to Gloria who grabs my hand and squeezes it.

"I think we're good. I hope today wasn't too upsetting for you," she says.

"You're not mad?" I ask.

"What should I be mad about? Stone explained everything to me."

"So you know nothing happened while she was a patient and that we also aren't seeing one another now. Our relationship is over."

"Well, I don't know about that. You two just need to talk." She turns to the group. "Okay, everybody, say goodbye. We need to get back to Elite." She turns back to me. "Since you drove separately, why don't you stay longer and talk to Stone?"

"Wait a minute. Did you plan this? The bus really isn't full, is it?" I ask. She shrugs and waves as she walks toward the exit with the group. I believe I've just been duped.

Stone walks over to me and sits down after saying goodbye to her teammates. "I'm glad you stayed behind. I want to talk and I need to do a lot of apologizing."

"You were the biggest asshole to me." My voice sounds a little too shaky, a little too emotional right now so I take a deep breath to steady myself. I still can't look at her.

"I know and I'm very sorry. I need to explain myself better," she says.

"How could you let somebody like Alison dictate your own feelings? Were they so weak for me to begin with?" I try to mask my emotions, but I know I'm failing.

She reaches for my hand, but I don't let her take it. "You have to understand something. You're my first attempt at a real relationship. I don't know how to love somebody. I don't know the steps to take and I'm vulnerable. I think I'm doing everything wrong. When Alison showed up that night, I was taken by surprise. She professed this need for you that I thought I could never compete with. She was very convincing. I'm sorry I let her get to me."

I finally look at her. "Why didn't you talk to me?" I wipe away the first tear.

"Because I'm a jerk and figured the easiest way was to cut all ties. I shut down when my feelings become too much for me to handle. I know that's a horrible excuse. It killed me to hurt you. It killed me. But I thought that was the best for you." She reaches out for my hand again.

I remain stiff, but I don't pull away from her. "You really hurt me."

She stands up and pulls me up so that I'm practically in her arms. "If you give us another chance, I promise to make it up to you. At least think about it. I know this is a lot to digest at once." She kisses my forehead and holds me until I lose some of my stiffness. I don't want to make this easy for her. This emotional up and down has been so hard for me. "I have to go and get ready for the game tonight. Please say you'll talk to me later." She tilts my chin up so that I have no choice but to look at her. "Please."

"Call me this weekend when you have time." I won't kiss her. I'm not even going to hug her. This is a big step for me.

"I'll take it, Doc."

❖

Can I come over after my game on Sunday?

I look at the clock. It's almost time for the game to start. I fall back on the couch, completely exhausted from today. It was good, then bad, then good, then scary, then good. It's almost seven and I'm seriously considering going to bed. If I agree to see Stone on Sunday, I'll have two days to clean up and prepare myself emotionally for her.

I take a deep breath before I answer her. *After your game?*

Yes, please. I can bring dinner, too.

I wait several seconds before answering her. If I agree to this, I'm opening myself up to get hurt the same way. If I don't, I have to walk away from Stone for good. I can't keep doing this. *Yes.* What can I say? I'm weak.

Thank you.

I don't hear from her the rest of the night. I check the score online and find out the Gray Wolves won the game six to three with Stone scoring half of the goals. I'm proud of her. She's having one of her best seasons ever. I think the injury really put things into perspective and she discovered an even greater love of the sport. Maybe this weekend I should study a little hockey, I mean, especially if we're going to try to make this work.

The rest of the weekend is spent cleaning and organizing. Even though I tell myself we aren't going to have sex, I wash my bedding and all of my delicates. Even if I wear practical clothing, I'm going to have something sexy on underneath. I call Rachel who encourages me to at least give Stone another chance. She knows I was upset, but also knows I cared a lot about Stone. By Sunday morning, I'm pacing. All of my laundry is done, I've dusted, vacuumed, scrubbed, and polished every single inch of the house. I still have four hours to kill, but I'm too wired to nap. I force myself to sit down and read the latest lesfic romance. If I can't have it in my real life, I can at least read about it.

I jump when I hear my phone buzz.

Are you still good with me coming over later? It's Stone and it's after five. I must have fallen asleep.

That's fine. What time are you thinking?
Is six okay?
That will give me about forty-five minutes to get myself ready. *Yes.*

I jump up and head straight for the shower. I won't have time to dry and curl my hair, but a nice long, hot shower will do me good. I can't believe I fell asleep for so long. I decide to wear jeans and a long sleeve button-down shirt with the sleeves rolled to my elbows. I put my hair in a messy bun and forgo socks. This is casual. This is how my Sunday would be even without Stone. I turn on the fireplace for added warmth. It's gas, but functional and gives the room a nice glow. I sit down and wait.

I hear a car pull up and my heart starts racing. I can feel heat spread inside of me as I wait for her to knock on the door. It's a quiet, hesitant knock. I put my hand on the door and take a deep breath before I open it.

"Hi."

I melt at her crooked smile with the faint dimple in her left cheek. "Come in."

She hands me a giant bag of takeout. "I've got two more things to carry in." She disappears down the stairs and returns with a heavy plastic tub. She carefully sets it down.

"Can I open it?" I ask. She holds up a finger and leaves again. "What are you doing?" I can't see out in the dark so I head to the kitchen to serve dinner. Smelling the food makes me realize how hungry I am. I turn around to find Stone behind me, her coat zipped up all the way. "Can I get you something to drink?" She has the weirdest look on her face, but the cutest smile. I can't help but smile, too. "What? What's going on?"

Stone gasps then giggles. She unzips her leather coat, reaches inside, and pulls out the tiniest gray and white kitten with eyes as blue as hers. "If we're going to start over, I don't want you to be lonely on the weekends I'm not in town. Apple will keep you company when I can't. She's very sweet and lovable. I think she's perfect for you."

"Oh! She's beautiful. You named her Apple. It's perfect. She's perfect. Thank you so much." I can't stop the tears in my eyes or the smile on my face. I take Apple and she reaches up to play with a strand of my hair. Without thinking, I lean forward and kiss Stone.

"So does this mean you're going to give us another chance?" She's serious.

I hold her chin and bring her lips close to mine. "Do you promise to always talk to me before you do something that alters this relationship?" She nods. "And promise to trust me over any of my ex-girlfriends or ex-fiancées?"

"Oh, my God. How many do you have of each?" That actually makes me laugh.

"Only one ex-fiancée and four ex-girlfriends." I hold up my hand when I see her start to count hers. "I don't need to know. Ever. This is a clean slate. From here on out. No excessive flirting, no phone numbers, just us. And Apple. Is that okay?"

"That sounds perfect," she says. Apple reaches up to play with a button on Stone's shirt.

"She has blue eyes like you do."

"They might change when she gets older, but I did it on purpose. That way, when I'm traveling, you can look at Apple and think of me."

"Wait. We need to get her set up. I need a litter box, toys, food." I start to panic now that I'm suddenly responsible for another living thing. Stone gets up and opens the Tupperware container, pulling out everything I just mentioned.

"She loves this kitten food. And this stuffed candy cane is her favorite toy." Stone shakes the toy until the tiny bell on it jingles. Apple stands up and stares at Stone, waiting for her to give her the toy or throw it. Stone tosses it on the couch and Apple, in all of her adorable awkwardness, hops over to it. She pounces on it and flips over, candy cane held high in her front paws. "We need to figure out where to put the litter box so she knows. What do you think?"

"Not the bedroom or out here. What about the hall bathroom?"

Stone nods and sets up the litter box in the corner of the bathroom. She gently wrangles Apple away from the toy and carries her down the hall to the litter box.

"It might be a good idea to close off the rest of the house so she can remember where her bathroom is." Stone shuts the office door, my bedroom door, and the guest room before she places Apple in the litter box. Apple starts digging around in the litter and relieves herself. "And now she's potty trained."

"Just like that?" I can't believe it's that easy.

"Just like that," Stone says. We watch as Apple investigates the bathroom and starts playing with the toilet paper. "That might become a problem." Stone quickly removes the paper and hides it in the cabinet.

Apple comes over to me and crawls up my jeans, her tiny nails scraping my leg. I'm so delighted she's this comfortable with me. I pick her up when she gets close to my pockets and we head back into the living room.

"Where should we put her little bed?" I ask.

Stone laughs. "Chances are she'll only use it tonight. Once she figures out where you sleep, she'll be right there with you." She hands me the tiny, fluffy bed and I put it on the couch next to where I normally sit. I place a very sleepy kitten on it. She drags her body to one of the corners and curls up.

"How long will she sleep?" I stare at Apple, already so in love.

"Hopefully for hours. Let her sleep for a little bit. Now we can finally talk," Stone says.

Chapter Thirty-nine

That sobers me up.
"Good idea." I lean back on the couch and watch as Stone closes the gap between us.

"Were you at a game a few weeks ago? Sitting in one of the boxes?"

"Yeah, with my friend Rachel. She, the other lesbian on Earth who doesn't know hockey, wanted to see you." I might as well tell the truth.

"I saw you. I was completely shocked and completely jealous. I thought maybe you were rubbing a new girlfriend in my face," she says.

I reach out and hold her hand. "I wouldn't do that. Rachel is just a friend. You're going to like her." I rub my thumb up and down the back of her fingers.

"She's very pretty," Stone says.

"She is, but I'm not attracted to her. After being at the game, she asked me if I thought it was worth dating a hockey player."

"What did you tell her?"

"At the time, we agreed it wasn't ideal, but obviously things have changed so I would probably tell her something different now. Although the players are young, something both of us failed to recognize at the time," I say.

She pulls my hand to her lips to kiss my fingertips. "I'm not too young for you, right?"

"Not at all. Besides, you're the oldest one on the team, right? Well, besides your coach."

Stone laughs. "I'm the second oldest on the team. Unless she likes dating baby dykes, then she probably shouldn't waste her time. How about we talk about us and less about Rachel? At least right now."

"You're right. Tell me what you want out of us."

"I want to have you in my life. I want to know that you're my rock and we're there for one another. I want to go out and do things with you, share hockey, work out, do things you like, do things I like. I want to fall asleep with you and wake up with you. I want to talk about everything and learn from one another. I want a girlfriend. I want a lover. I want a best friend. I want that to be you, Hayley."

"I want all of that, too. Can you just promise me that we will always talk about things? I can't have you pull away like that."

She leans forward and kisses me softly. "I promise I will never do that again." She continues to kiss me and within a matter of moments, it becomes heated and I pull her on top of me, anxious to feel her body against mine.

"I've missed you so much, Elizabeth," I whisper. She leans up to look into my eyes. She touches my face, slowly and softly. I release the last of my hesitation. Stone is who I want. She is my everything. I stare into her beautiful eyes and I know she's the one. "I love you." I see surprise register on her face and the line on her forehead deepens. I reach up and rub it smooth. "It's not supposed to confuse you. It's supposed to make you happy." She leans down so that I can't see her face, but I feel the tear that lands on my cheek. I hold her even closer. "Don't cry." She shakes her head at me. I feel another tear and another. I gently, but firmly pull her chin up so I can look into her eyes.

"I'm crying because I'm so happy. You took me back after I was horrible to you, and now you tell me that you love me. What did I do to deserve you?"

"Stop. All of that is in the past, remember? Today is a new start for us as long as you want it."

"Of course I want it. I want this, you, us, more than anything." I try to wipe her tears away, but she stands up out of my reach. "Come here, I want to show you something." She gently pulls me down the hall and opens the door to my bedroom.

"What about Apple?"

"She'll be asleep for at least an hour. That gives us some much needed alone time." She kisses me as we walk to the bed, her fingers quickly unbuttoning my shirt.

I slip my hands under her shirt, anxious to feel her warmth again. "I've missed you so much."

That gets her to speed up. She pulls us onto the bed and backs away only to shed her clothes and rip off my jeans. My white lacy panties and bra stop her for just a moment. "You're so beautiful, Doc. I've missed everything about you. Your taste, your touch. I love you so much and I'm going to spend the rest of my life making sure you know that." She crawls back between my legs and runs her tongue from my neck, down between my breasts, over my stomach and grabs my hips to lift them up so that her mouth is on my mound.

"Stone, Stone. Take them off." I want her mouth on my skin, not on my panties. She isn't gentle when she rips them off, tearing them in the process. It's so hot and I'm so desperate for her, that I don't even care. I moan deeply when her mouth finally finds me. "I've missed you and your mouth so much." I buck into her, wanting more. She slips two fingers inside of me. I lift my hips up and down, greedy for her. She holds me down with her free hand and resumes her glorious torture of my wet center. I come twice in a row.

"I've missed us so much." She takes off the rest of her clothes until we're both finally naked. I reach out for her immediately. She flips us so that I'm on top. I straddle her waist and look down at her. I see love and trust in her eyes. She reaches up and runs her fingers over my breasts. I lean back and moan. "You're still so wet." She bucks her hips up and into me and I smile.

"This feels nice," I say. She gyrates her hips and I moan again. "Really nice."

"I can do something about that later," she says. I lift an eyebrow at her. "Come here and kiss me."

I lean down and stretch myself against her. "You're so warm. And you have a certain spicy and sweet smell that I love." I slide down her body, gently biting and touching all the way down to the junction of her thighs. I spread her with my hands and taste her again.

Her hips press into me and I feel her hand at the back of my head, keeping me in place. She wants to come fast. We can go slower later. I carefully slip a finger inside her, amazed at her tightness. Her slick walls contract against me. I'm almost afraid to move inside of her, afraid I'm going to hurt her. Her moans tell me otherwise. I find her clit and lick and suck her until I feel her legs starting to shake. I slowly move my finger and she cries out when she climaxes. I can't believe Stone is mine. This glorious, beautiful woman wants to be with me. I almost cry again. Instead, I make my way back up Stone's body, dropping kisses along the way. She pulls me close to her, wraps her arms around me, and we fall asleep almost immediately.

❖

Why is Stone scratching me? I'm groggy and open my eyes because whatever she is doing is no longer playful, but kind of annoying. Apple has found her way between us and is tangled in my hair. I smile.

"What's going on?" Stone croaks out.

"Our little Apple found us and wants to play," I say.

Stone groans in response. "Is this what it's going to be like when we have kids?"

My heart skips a few beats. "Apparently. This is no different than if you wanted to play." I playfully poke Stone in the back.

She rolls over so she is facing us. "Apple, we did not agree on this. You were supposed to help me get the girl and then sleep the night away, not interrupt our sleep. We had a deal, munchkin." Stone reaches out and pets Apple's head. She falls down and offers Stone her belly instead. "Look at you. So much like your mom already."

I bust out laughing. "I thought you liked me like that."

"Oh, very much so. You're absolute perfection." She leans over Apple to kiss me, then kisses Apple on her tummy. "I love us."

"I love us, too. Do you want to know when I fell in love with you?" She nods. "In my kitchen, when you kissed me senseless and said you couldn't wait to taste me. I fell in love with your passion, your mouth, the way you made me feel so desirable."

"Do you want to know what made me fall in love with you?" It's my turn to nod. She takes one of my hands and brings it to her lips. "I fell in love with you because of your gentleness, your honesty." She pauses for emphasis. "And everything about your touch."

About the Author

Kris Bryant grew up a military brat living in several different countries before her family settled down in the Midwest when she was twelve. Books were her only form of entertainment overseas, and she read anything and everything within her reach. Reading eventually turned into writing when she decided she didn't like the way some of the novels ended and wanted to give the characters she fell in love with the ending she thought they so deserved.

Earning a B.A. in English from the University of Missouri, Kris focused more on poetry, and after some encouragement from her girlfriend, decided to tackle her own book.

Kris can be contacted at krisbryantbooks@gmail.com

Website: http://www.krisbryant.net

Books Available from Bold Strokes Books

Between Sand and Stardust by Tina Michele. Are the lifelong bonds of love strong enough to conquer time, distance, and heartache when Haven Thorne and Willa Bennette are given another chance at forever? (978-1-62639-940-2)

Charming the Vicar by Jenny Frame. When magician and atheist Finn Kane seeks refuge in an English village after a spiritual crisis, can local vicar Bridget Claremont restore her faith in life and love? (978-1-63555-029-0)

Data Capture by Jesse J. Thoma. Lola Walker is undercover on the hunt for cybercriminals while trying not to notice the woman who might be perfectly wrong for her for all the right reasons. (978-1-62639-985-3)

Epicurean Delights by Renee Roman. Ariana Marks had no idea a leisure swim would lead to being rescued, in more ways than one, by the charismatic Hudson Frost. (978-1-63555-100-6)

Heart of the Devil by Ali Vali. We know most of Cain and Emma Casey's story, but *Heart of the Devil* will take you back to where it began one fateful night with a tray loaded with beer. (978-1-63555-045-0)

Known Threat by Kara A. McLeod. When Special Agent Ryan O'Connor reluctantly questions who protects the Secret Service, she learns courage truly is found in unlikely places. Agent O'Connor Series #3 (978-1-63555-132-7)

Seer and the Shield by D. Jackson Leigh. Time is running out for the Dragon Horse Army while two unlikely heroines struggle to put aside their attraction and find a way to stop a deadly cult. Dragon Horse War, Book 3 (978-1-63555-170-9)

Sinister Justice by Steve Pickens. When a vigilante targets citizens of Jake Finnigan's hometown, Jake and his partner Sam fall under suspicion themselves as they investigate the murders. (978-1-63555-094-8)

The Universe Between Us by Jane C. Esther. Ana Mitchell must make the hardest choice of her life: the promise of new love Jolie Dann on Earth, or a humanity-saving mission to colonize Mars. (978-1-63555-106-8)

Touch by Kris Bryant. Can one touch heal a heart? (978-1-63555-084-9)

Change in Time by Robyn Nyx. Working in the past is hell on your future. The Extractor series: Book Two. (978-1-62639-880-1)

Love After Hours by Radclyffe. When Gina Antonelli agrees to renovate Carrie Longmire's new house, she doesn't welcome Carrie's overtures at friendship or her own unexpected attraction. A Rivers Community Novel. (978-1-63555-090-0)

Nantucket Rose by CF Frizzell. Maggie Jordan can't wait to convert an historic Nantucket home into a B&B, but doesn't expect to fall for mariner Ellis Chilton, who has more claim to the house than Maggie realizes. (978-1-63555-056-6)

Picture Perfect by Lisa Moreau. Falling in love wasn't supposed to be part of the stakes for Olive and Gabby, rival photographers in the competition of a lifetime. (978-1-62639-975-4)

Set the Stage by Karis Walsh. Actress Emilie Danvers takes the stage again in Ashland, Oregon, little realizing that landscaper Arden Philips is about to offer her a very personal romantic lead role. (978-1-63555-087-0)

Strike a Match by Fiona Riley. When their attempts at matchmaking fizzle out, firefighter Sasha and reluctant millionairess Abby find themselves turning to each other to strike a perfect match. (978-1-62639-999-0)

The Price of Cash by Ashley Bartlett. Cash Braddock is doing her best to keep her business afloat, stay out of jail, and avoid Detective Kallen. It's not working. (978-1-62639-708-8)

Under Her Wing by Ronica Black. At Angel's Wings Rescue, dogs are usually the ones saved, but when quiet Kassandra Haden meets outspoken owner Jayden Beaumont, the two stubborn women just might end up saving each other. (978-1-63555-077-1)

Underwater Vibes by Mickey Brent. When Hélène, a translator in Brussels, Belgium, meets Sylvie, a young Greek photographer and swim coach, unsettling feelings hijack Hélène's mind and body—even her poems. (978-1-63555-002-3)

A More Perfect Union by Carsen Taite. Major Zoey Granger and DC fixer Rook Daniels risk their reputations for a chance at true love while dealing with a scandal that threatens to rock the military. (978-1-62639-754-5)

Arrival by Gun Brooke. The spaceship *Pathfinder* reaches its passengers' new homeworld where danger lurks in the shadows while Pamas Seclan disembarks and finds unexpected love in young science genius Darmiya Do Voy. (978-1-62639-859-7)

Captain's Choice by VK Powell. Architect Kerstin Anthony's life is going to plan until Bennett Carlyle, the first girl she ever kissed, is assigned to her latest and most important project, a police district substation. (978-1-62639-997-6)

Falling Into Her by Erin Zak. Pam Phillips, widow at the age of forty, meets Kathryn Hawthorne, local Chicago celebrity, and it changes her life forever—in ways she hadn't even considered possible. (978-1-63555-092-4)

Hookin' Up by MJ Williamz. Will Leah get what she needs from casual hookups or will she see the love she desires right in front of her? (978-1-63555-051-1)

King of Thieves by Shea Godfrey. When art thief Casey Marinos meets bounty hunter Finnegan Starkweather, the crimes of the past just might set the stage for a payoff worth more than she ever dreamed possible. (978-1-63555-007-8)

Lucy's Chance by Jackie D. As a serial killer haunts the streets, Lucy tries to stitch up old wounds with her first love in the wake of a small town's rapid descent into chaos. (978-1-63555-027-6)

Right Here, Right Now by Georgia Beers. When Alicia Wright moves into the office next door to Lacey Chamberlain's accounting firm, Lacey is about to find out that sometimes the last person you want is exactly the person you need. (978-1-63555-154-9)

Strictly Need to Know by MB Austin. Covert operator Maji Rios will do whatever she must to complete her mission, but saving a gorgeous stranger from Russian mobsters was not in her plans. (978-1-63555-114-3)

Tailor-Made by Yolanda Wallace. Tailor Grace Henderson doesn't date clients, but when she meets gender-bending model Dakota Lane, she's tempted to throw all the rules out the window. (978-1-63555-081-8)

Time Will Tell by M. Ullrich. With the ability to time travel, Eva Caldwell will have to decide between having it all and erasing it all. (978-1-63555-088-7)

A Date to Die by Anne Laughlin. Someone is killing people close to Detective Kay Adler, who must look to her own troubled past for a suspect. There she finds more than one person seeking revenge against her. (978-1-63555-023-8)

Captured Soul by Laydin Michaels. Can Kadence Munroe save the woman she loves from a twisted killer, or will she lose her to a collector of souls? (978-1-62639-915-0)

Dawn's New Day by TJ Thomas. Can Dawn Oliver and Cam Cooper, two women who have loved and lost, open their hearts to love again? (978-1-63555-072-6)

Definite Possibility by Maggie Cummings. Sam Miller is just out for good times, but Lucy Weston makes her realize happily ever after is a definite possibility. (978-1-62639-909-9)

Eyes Like Those by Melissa Brayden. Isabel Chase and Taylor Andrews struggle between love and ambition from the writers' room on one of Hollywood's hottest TV shows. (978-1-63555-012-2)

Heart's Orders by Jaycie Morrison. Helen Tucker and Tee Owens escape hardscrabble lives to careers in the Women's Army Corps, but more than their hearts are at risk as friendship blossoms into love. (978-1-63555-073-3)

Hiding Out by Kay Bigelow. Treat Dandridge is unaware that her life is in danger from the murderer who is hunting the woman she's falling in love with, Mickey Heiden. (978-1-62639-983-9)

Omnipotence Enough by Sophia Kell Hagin. Can the tiny tool that abducted war veteran Jamie Gwynmorgan accidentally acquires help her escape an unknown enemy to reclaim her stolen life and the woman she deeply loves? (978-1-63555-037-5)

Summer's Cove by Aurora Rey. Emerson Lange moved to Provincetown to live in the moment, but when she meets Darcy Belo and her son Liam, her quest for summer romance becomes a family affair. (978-1-62639-971-6)

The Road to Wings by Julie Tizard. Lieutenant Casey Tompkins, Air Force student pilot, has to fly with the toughest instructor, Captain Kathryn "Hard Ass" Hardesty, fly a supersonic jet, and deal with a growing forbidden attraction. (978-1-62639-988-4)

Beauty and the Boss by Ali Vali. Ellis Renois is at the top of the fashion world, but she never expects her summer assistant Charlotte Hamner to tear her heart and her business apart like sharp scissors through cheap material. (978-1-62639-919-8)

Fury's Choice by Brey Willows. When gods walk amongst humans, can two women find a balance between love and faith? (978-1-62639-869-6)

Lessons in Desire by MJ Williamz. Can a summer love stand a four-month hiatus and still burn hot? (978-1-63555-019-1)

Lightning Chasers by Cass Sellars. For Sydney and Parker, being a couple was never what they had planned. Now they have to fight corruption, murder, and enemies hiding in plain sight just to hold on to each other. Lightning Series, Book Two. (978-1-62639-965-5)

Summer Fling by Jean Copeland. Still jaded from a breakup years earlier, Kate struggles to trust falling in love again when a summer fling with sexy young singer Jordan rocks her off her feet. (978-1-62639-981-5)

Take Me There by Julie Cannon. Adrienne and Sloan know it would be career suicide to mix business with pleasure, however tempting it is. But what's the harm? They're both consenting adults. Who would know? (978-1-62639-917-4)

The Girl Who Wasn't Dead by Samantha Boyette. A year ago, someone tried to kill Jenny Lewis. Tonight she's ready to find out who it was. (978-1-62639-950-1)

Unchained Memories by Dena Blake. Can a woman give herself completely when she's left a piece of herself behind? (978-1-62639-993-8)

Walking Through Shadows by Sheri Lewis Wohl. All Molly wanted to do was go backpacking…in her own century. (978-1-62639-968-6)

Lightning Source UK Ltd.
Milton Keynes UK
UKOW04f1856151217
314562UK00001B/59/P